REED

Bowen Boys Book 6

KATHI S. BARTON

WCP

World Castle Publishing, LLC
Pesacola, Florida

Copyright © Kathi S. Barton 2014
Print ISBN: 9781629891743
eBook ISBN: 9781629891750
First Edition World Castle Publishing, LLC, November 28, 2014
http://www.worldcastlepublishing.com

Licensing Notes

Cover: Karen Fuller
Editor: Eric Johnston
Editor: Maxine Bringenberg

CHAPTER 1

Kerry reached for the phone when it rang. There were others in the room with her, but she doubted that any of them were paying attention to the monitors. As soon as she answered, the man at the other end started screaming at her. She picked up the little ball on her desk and played with it until he calmed down. Or took a breath.

"Are you fucking listening to me?"

"I am, even though by rights you should have been hung up on when I first answered; so yes, I'm still listening to you." She smiled when he started cursing again.

"So what the hell are you going to do about it then?"

"I'm assuming this is over your cable being shut off." He told her it fucking was. "Well, I can take a payment now and it will be on within the next twenty-four to forty —"

"I want it fucking back on now." She waited while he went on another cussing tirade. "I have people here that have come to watch the fight that's on tonight, not two days from now. Turn it on and I'll pay you in the morning."

"No." He was quiet for a few seconds, and then started in on her parentage as well as her level of intelligence before she cut him off. "I'm sorry about your company, sir, but you've received numerous calls from us as well as two

5

bills. As of right now, your cable bill is past due by nearly four months. You'll need to make a payment before service can be turned back on."

"I never received a bill." She rolled her eyes and bounced her ball against the monitor. Kerry could see in front of her that he had called last month and made arrangements to pay, which he had not done. As she started to tell him this a note was put on her desk. Kerry looked at it, then at the man who stood waiting. A little afraid now, she decided that the note was much more important than the abuse she was receiving from the man, and cut him off again.

"You've received enough bills to have you call in last month and try to make arrangements to pay it off. You were to pay half by that Friday and then the other half over the next two months. The only thing I can tell you now, sir, is that it will need to be paid in full before any of the services can be turned back on." He started to scream at her again and she disconnected the call, something she wished she'd done before when he'd cursed at her.

"Why do they want me to come now?" The other customer service rep shrugged. She stood up, took off her headphones, and looked at the front offices, then sat back down and looked at him again. He shrugged again and walked away from her. When he was gone, she picked up her things—all of the toys and other things that were hers on the desk—and shoved them into her backpack. If she was going to be fired, she wasn't going to have them pack up her shit and send it to her. She was taking it now. Grabbing the three pens that were also hers, she debated on whether to take the framed awards, and thought how little good they'd do her if she was terminated. She went to her boss's office and knocked on his door.

"You wanted to see me?" He nodded and motioned for her to come in. She couldn't stand this man. Robbie Kline was a pompous ass, and he lorded his position over all of them like he was king and not a simple lead. She had told him on more than one occasion that he'd only gotten his job because she hadn't wanted it. She supposed that was what made him hate her so much.

"I'm supposed to tell you that—" Marvin Simon stepped into the room with them and she stood up. Now this man she liked. When he told her to sit down, she did so and they both looked at Robbie. "I thought I was going to tell her."

"Well, you are. I'm just here in the event she has any questions. Do you?" She looked at Marvin, then at Robbie, confused. "Ah, he's not told you yet. Good. That lets me do it."

Robbie started to speak and was cut off with a look from his boss. Marvin had two looks...one that made you feel like he'd cut your throat when he was pissed, and another that said he was very proud of you. She'd never seen the first, but apparently what others said about it was true. It was fucking scary.

"You're being promoted." She looked at Robbie, who glared before looking back at Marvin. "You still want to be on the outside, don't you? I wouldn't actually call it a promotion, but since you want to do this, I'm sure you'll think of it as one. I'm going to miss you."

"I'm going to get to lay lines?" He nodded at her, and she gripped the arms of the chair tighter, waiting for him to tell her that he was kidding. "You can start training Monday morning. I've asked that you be set up with someone knowledgeable, but I don't know them as well as I do my service reps. I'm just hoping that if you hate it, you come back to me. Your job is—"

Kerry stood up and hugged him. He stood as well and hugged her back. Robbie snorted but neither of them paid any attention to him. She didn't care; she was going to be able to be outside instead of stuck in the office all the time. Kerry Stephens was going to be a lineman.

She went back to her desk to clean it up after getting the rundown on what she was going to be doing and how she should dress, and receiving several books from Marvin to look at over the long weekend. Kerry was given the rest of the day off and into the weekend to get ready to move to another shift. She'd been working nights for so long that she wasn't sure what to do about seeing the sun. Grinning, she took the awards off her cubicle and put them into her bag with the rest of her things she was going to abandon. The little ball that had helped her with stress was still in her hand when she went to the door.

"You leaving early? Got yourself a new position and now you're cutting out before your time? Shame on you." She ignored Robbie and smiled at the guard at the door, who was checking her bag. "You know that you'll be back, don't you? As soon as you do, I'm going to laugh my ass off at you for the failure that we both know that you are."

He'd hurt her, and as much as she tried to hide it, she was sure he'd seen it. She wasn't a failure, but he'd made her feel like one every day of the past ten years she'd worked here. She turned to him when the guard handed back her bag.

"You're a sad, sad man, Robbie. I hope that someday your mouth catches up with you and someone puts you in your place." She turned to leave only to have him grab her arm. She looked at him until he let her go.

"You think you're going to be this big bad lineman and that you'll be able to come back here and kick my ass? Get real. You're nothing but a female, and at the first sign of trouble, you'll be back."

"No, I won't, because I won't fail. It's not in me to fail. I could come back and beat your ass, but I'm not going to waste my time in trying to teach you a lesson you should have learned a long time ago."

"Oh yeah, and what lesson do you think that might be? Respect?" He snorted. "I don't show you respect because we both know that you're well beneath me. Someday I'm going to own this company, and when I do, what do you think is going to happen then?"

"Not much of anything, because by then hell would have frozen over." She laughed with the guard and walked out the door. Robbie was telling him to shut the fuck up as the door closed behind her. Kerry had to control the urge to skip all the way to her car. She was that fucking happy.

The first person she called was her sister. "I got the job. I'm going to be a lineman starting Monday."

She knew the moment her sister didn't say anything that she was having another drama. Dora didn't really care that whatever it was could be fixed. It was all the same to her. Something for her to complain about and whine about.

"Will you make more money?" Kerry sat in her car and closed her eyes, wishing now she hadn't called. "I could use a loan to tide me over until you get the next commission check. I'm all out of money for rent."

"I won't have any more commission checks, Dora. I told you that before. And I paid your rent two weeks ago. Where is that money?" She'd been in a hurry and not paid the landlord directly this time. "You didn't pay the rent with it, did you?"

"I have needs, little sister, and the rent was not one of them at the time you gave it to me. I've told you before that you need to set me up on your account so that I can have access to your checking account, and I'd never have to bother you again about this shit." She heard someone talking and knew it was the boyfriend again. "Death says to tell you that the sooner the better."

Enough was enough. She was finished with her sister and her boyfriends. She'd told her this before and now she really was finished. She had a job she liked and she needed to start caring for herself, and not her sister who was too fucking lazy to not only find a job but to keep one.

"Look, Dora, I'm not giving you money and I'm not going to give you access to my account. Not now and not ever. And as of right now, I'm not bailing your ass out every time you think you—"

"You will too. If you don't, I'm going to tell Daddy." Kerry closed her eyes. "What do you think he'd say if you left us without a place to stay? Huh? You think he'd be happy with you? No, he loves me and wants the best for me."

"I'm finished." She closed her phone and then reached for it again after she tossed it on the seat next to her. She pressed down hard on the off button and was glad when it asked her if she wanted to power off. She most certainly did. She started her car and went to see her dad. He was on her shit list too.

~~~

Reed watched the numbers fly across his screen. He was looking for one in particular, and when it popped up three times in a row, he paused. There she was. He wrote down the times as well as the number it had come from and put this information on the chart he'd set up for this case.

He glanced up when his sister-in-law, Caitlynne, sat down across from him.

"You should have cleaned out your desk a week ago, Reed. What the hell are you doing now?" He grinned at her, and Caitlynne, his boss up until three weeks ago, grinned back. "You found it, didn't you?"

"Yeah. I found some of them yesterday, and then today this whole other set of papers came across my desk. I couldn't leave it alone and decided to have a look." He handed her the files. "She's been calling again. Not a lot at first, but more over the past few days. Monday is not her usual day to call in deals."

Caitlynne looked them over, then handed them back to him. "You think you can work this for us when we get back to Ohio? I know that once we get back we're going to be fairly bored. I'm actually looking forward to being a simple chief of police with my trusty brother-in-law as my sidekick."

Reed laughed and began the process of shutting down his computer. It was all he had left to pack up. He stuffed his things in his bag and stood up and looked around. He'd only been on temporary assignment here with her, and was actually looking forward to going back home permanently too. However, he was going to miss this.

"I'm glad you decided to come and work with me. Hopefully we'll get some things done while we're together. Our little town will be the safest in the world when we roll into it." He laughed when she did. "Are you okay with this?"

"Yes. I've signed on the house I've wanted forever. I've ordered furniture that's going to be delivered tomorrow, and the housekeeper and cook start today to get things where they want them. Thank you, by the way, for letting

Camps come and be with me. That guy is amazing." They moved to the elevator and he had his badge ready to turn in when he left. "Are you sure about this?"

"I'm not going to lie to you. I'm going to miss it a great deal, but being home sounds good too. It's been a long time since I've been able to relax there and not worry every time the phone rang who'd been murdered. Walker is happy too. He and Khan have the clinic all set up and patients already coming to see him."

They were riding to the airport together. Everything he'd wanted to take back with him had already been moved and put on board. As soon as they were seated, the pilot told them that they'd be moving in a few minutes. Reed took the glass of tea when the stewardess handed it to him.

"Mom and Dad said their house was going to be done soon. I was hoping they'd have it done before Christmas. I'm glad it will be." He'd wanted Christmas at their old home, but the foundation had been bad and the house that they'd grown up in was now rubble. But they sounded happy about the one that they had now.

"The cable company was out Friday when I left there to finish up here. They were supposed to come back today and install and lay the lines. Your dad is having a good time telling everyone that he was going to have a wireless house. Do you suppose he has any idea what that means?" Reed told her he didn't think so. "I swear to you the next time George says 'shit,' I'm going to hunt your father down and beat him."

Reed laughed, and didn't mention that he knew that Jack was teaching him the word and that Ama was teaching him to spit. He was getting pretty good at it too. He leaned back in his chair and thought of the things he was having done to his house.

Tomorrow he was going to run in his back yard. Closing his eyes, he smiled when he thought of how big it was. Caitlynne had helped him with the down payment on the place, and he was both scared and nervous about owing her and Walker so much. But he also knew that once he was able to make his first half year of payments he'd be able to pay them back. The bank had asked that he leave the money he'd been saving for the house in the accounts until the first six months went by. Being that he didn't have a great deal of credit to his name he'd needed a co-signer. Walker and Caitlynne had come through for him, and now he had his dream house.

When he got home today, he was going to find himself a bed. He'd had a nice one at Caitlynne's when he'd stayed there, and he'd even done research on it. Reed was nothing if not thorough. Thinking about trying out the different mattresses in the stores had him smiling at one particular memory involving a sales woman and her...commission. Reed opened his eyes when Caitlynne laughed.

"I don't suppose you're thinking about how much you're looking forward to a hug from your mom and dad, are you?" She laughed harder when he flushed. "I didn't think so. Is sex all you Bowen boys think about?"

"Most men in general, I suppose. What about you? You never think about it?" The two of them had had a great many conversations that would probably seem odd to others if they knew. "Women aren't as visual as men, I've heard. Maybe we just are more...I don't know, maybe we're more romantic than you."

She snorted at him and laughed. "I highly doubt that. Walker is. And I've seen Dylan be romantic, but the rest...? Not so much. George is; I've seen him bring home flowers for Corrine when he just wanted to. That's really nice. And he takes her places he doesn't enjoy."

"Like the opera." She nodded. "I actually think he enjoys it more than he says. I heard him telling Khan about the last one they went to, and he sounded like he had more fun than Mom."

The pilot asked them to buckle up, that they'd be landing soon. He was putting his belt on when he thought of something. Well, he'd been thinking of it for several weeks, but only just now had her alone where he could ask her.

"Caitlynne, do you think that my mate will be something like the rest of you? I mean, will she be...?" He wanted to say bitchy, but was afraid of hurting her feelings. She seemed to get it.

"You mean a pain in your ass? Mouthy? How about not easy?" She nodded. "Yes, and so much more. And just so you know, we're all taking bets on how hard she's going to make you suffer when you do find her."

"Gee, thanks." He felt the plane touch down and closed his eyes. He hated this part of flying. He had no idea why it bothered him so much, but there it was.

When they were cleared to leave the plane, he wasn't surprised to see his entire family there waiting for him. But the only one he had eyes for was his favorite girl.

"Hello there, love." He picked up Abby and held her to him. She smelled like panther and baby powder. He smiled when she hugged him with her chubby little arms. Little Khan yanked on his pant leg and he picked him up too. George simply walked with them as if he didn't want any part of the three of them. But Reed knew that the little guy loved him too. Monica took Abby and Khan when he started for his luggage.

"We're having dinner at our house tonight, then tomorrow we're going over to the new house and try to make some sense of the things Mom and Dad had delivered." His dad huffed at Monica. "You're the one that wanted us to help you. I would just as soon stay out on the deck and pester you from there."

"I've never seen so much furniture in my life. I don't know why we had to have all new." Reed covered his mouth when his mother rolled her eyes. "We already had the bed and dressers. Why'd you have to go out and get something else?"

"Because, you old fool, I'm starting over. I can very well do that with a new mate too if you don't learn to shut up. Now, grab that bag there and let's get going. I, for one, am excited about tomorrow, and unless you want me to make you do something we both know you won't care for, then you'd better start thinking before you speak. I've got my family here now and I'm ready to keep them here."

They'd been having this same argument for years. If it wasn't something new, it was something that Mom had bought because whatever it had been was broken. Dad, of course, thought that everything could be fixed eventually and stored it in the garage. Lately, Mom had been, he knew, simply tossing the broken whatever and purchasing a replacement. She'd told him that the garage was full enough, thank you very much.

As soon as they were all loaded up, he turned to Khan. "I have to go by the house first. I've got some stuff going on there and want to see how it's progressing. I'll drive over. It shouldn't be but an hour tops."

"If you don't mind, I'll hang out with you." He looked at his brother oddly. "I want to talk to you about something. I've got...I just need to talk to you about it alone."

Reed nodded and tried to think what the hell could be so important that he wanted to speak to him alone. He watched his house come into view as they pulled into the drive, and smiled. Christ, this was going to be perfect.

CHAPTER 2

"What do you mean, I'll have to figure it out on my own?" Kerry looked at the orders she'd been handed when they left the office, then back at Russ McCall. "It's my first day. How the hell am I supposed to figure it out on my own?"

"You want to be a line person, you are going to have to figure it out by yourself. I'm not going to be a babysitter for you. You women should just answer the phone and let us men do the labor. Why the fuck do you want to be out here anyway?" He looked at her from his perch in the cab of the company truck. "I heard tell from Kline that you made a hell of a lot of money selling this shit. I'm thinking if you're so high and mighty on selling, you should have no problems installing it for your clients."

He'd made "client" sound like a dirty word. She stood there for a minute wondering why the hell she'd been assigned to him, when she knew that she was supposed to be with someone else. Marvin had called her last night and told her he'd set it all up for her. Now she had this man. And she knew for a fact, because she'd taken some of the calls, that he was the worst installer they had out there.

Gathering up the things she needed, or in this case thought she needed, she went to the house. There was a note on the door from the customer telling them to knock loudly, that they were in the basement. She looked back at Russ when he told her to get back to the truck.

"Come on, we're done here. We don't have to do anything special for them. They want it, they should have put it on the order." She knocked hard on the door. "Mother fuck. Do you know that if they aren't home or don't answer we can get off early? And still get paid? Well, you little bitch, you really are on your own."

He started the truck and pulled out of the drive. She was still staring at him when the woman came to the door. What the fuck was she supposed to do now?

"Hello. Thank so much for knocking so I can hear you. You've no idea how many times I've set this appointment up only to have missed the man." She opened the door. "Oh my, you're a girl."

"Yes, ma'am, I am. I've just...I need to make a call." She reached into her pocket only to remember that she'd left her things in the truck. She turned back to the woman and smiled. Now what?

The line had been delivered yesterday, so she had that. And thankfully the books she'd been given were an easy read for her...all of the manuals and such to take her test after her first week. She was glad now she'd taken the time over the weekend to read them over so she'd have at least some idea what she was doing.

The line was a lot heavier than she'd thought it would be, but she managed to get it up the pole, only dropping it twice. By the time she'd gotten herself up the stupid thing three times, she was glad that she'd taken everything from the truck with her, because she was going to die if she had to do this again.

After an hour she finally thought she had it hooked up. Coming down the pole was a great deal scarier than going up, as she had to make herself hold tighter because she was getting exhausted. Moving to the side of the house, the customer, Mrs. Mills, came out with a bottle of water.

"I saw you up there and couldn't believe how amazing you looked. How long have you worked for the cable company?" Kerry looked up at her and smiled. "A while I bet. You look like it."

She nodded and told her ten years. "It was my first job and I loved it. There's something so satisfying about helping out customers with their issues."

After draining the bottle, she set to work hooking the cables to the house. Lucky for her the house had had cable before, so all she needed to do was hook up the house and make sure that the jacks were hooked to the televisions. This order had nothing but the basics on it, and she was thankful.

After another hour and a half, she was just checking the last television when another truck pulled into the drive. She didn't bother seeing who it was because she thought it was Russ. When she started for the truck she saw Marvin leaning against it, frowning. Kerry turned back to Mrs. Mills.

"If you have any questions or concerns, please call the number on the order. And don't forget to call and ask about the phone service we talked about. I think you might save a bundle with having that over the one you have."

Mrs. Mills nodded and smiled, then looked at Marvin. "You her boss?"

Kerry looked over her shoulder, not realizing that Marvin had come up so close to them. He nodded and smiled.

"She did a great job today. I'm sure when you send her out on these new services that you know she's going to do so, but I always try to make sure when I've had exemplary service I let someone know. I'm telling you now that I'll get the rest of your products too because of her. Never had anyone so proud of their job before."

"Thank you very much, ma'am. It's always nice to hear good things about our employees." He shook Mrs. Mills's hand, then walked with Kerry back to his truck. "Where is Russ? And where is the truck?"

"I don't know to either question." She rolled the large roll of wire to the side of the house and began gathering her tools. "He said that he had...fuck him. I'm not going to try and cover for him. He left me here when we first got here. Said that Kline told him that I was making great money, and that he couldn't figure out why a woman was trying to do his job. I've not seen him since."

Marvin nodded. "So you did this all on your own without calling anyone? I don't suppose it occurred to you to call the office and let someone know."

She dumped her bag on the back of the truck and turned to him. "And just how was I supposed to manage that? By smoke signals? I wasn't worthy of touching the precious cell phone, and he took mine with him. My lunch and my water too. I don't know what the fuck I would have done had she not given me...." She took a deep breath. "I'm sorry. I'd like very much for someone to tell me if I'm fired or not."

"Why would I fire you?" She shrugged and got into the truck. He started it up and moved out of the drive before he continued. "Russ showed up at another site this morning, bragging to the other tech that he'd left you high and dry. He told the other man that he hoped you'd fail and then him and Kline were going to celebrate. What did he say about Kline?"

"He said that I had to figure it out on my own, that he wasn't a babysitter. He said that as a woman I should just answer the phone and let the men folk do the labor. He said that he'd heard from Kline that I was a top seller basically, and that since I sell so much that I should be able to install it." She leaned her head back against the seat. "I'm done and starved. I only had the one install today that I'm aware of."

"It was all I wanted you to do on your first day with David. But since you were with Russ, he had a great many more. I'm taking you to the office so you can report him." She started to shake her head when he told her to hush up. "You're not the first tech to have him do this to them. The last female we hired simply quit, and it wasn't until a month later that we heard he'd done about the same to her. I don't want him out here any longer, and I would like it if you'd help me with that."

She leaned back against the seat and thought about it. When she looked up again, he was pulling into a restaurant. Kerry had no money, but a fat juicy hamburger with all the trimmings sounded so good. When he pulled into a parking place, she reached for his hand when he started to get out.

"I can't do this. Not only do I have no money but...." She looked out the window. "I went to see my dad yesterday. He's broke again. Well, he's not now, but now I am. The power guy showed up as I was getting out of my car and I told him that this was it. I mean it this time. I'm buying me a house and keeping all my money for me."

"It's about time you learned to tell them to screw off." She shrugged, and he got out and told her to come with him. "This is my treat. I missed your birthday this year and I'll buy you lunch. Oh, by the way, I have your bag and phone."

"I didn't have a birthday yet this year." He handed her the cell phone as well as her bag. He didn't stop walking, and she had to run to keep up with him. "Marvin, I can't afford this even if I just got paid. Come on, I'll let you buy me a burger at the place down the street."

He stopped so suddenly that she bumped into him. When he turned to her, she knew that something more than lunch was going on. She looked at the front of the place then back at him. It took her a few minutes but she got it.

"Christ, they're here, aren't they? The big wigs are here and I'm going to report him now?" He nodded. "Damn it all to hell, Marvin, this is not fucking funny."

"When the prospective owners found out what happened today, I had…damn it, Russ was bragging about what he'd done to you in front of the lawyer and one of the family that bought us. Mr. Bowen immediately called his brother. He was not a happy person. We were supposed to be out on a grand tour and I was going to show them what an amazing group we had out in the fields and on the phones." He moved to the door and stood holding it open. "Kerry, I don't have to tell you what happens if this deal falls through. We're about the only independent cable company in the world, and they want to own us. Without them, we're toast. And they want to talk to you."

She looked at him, then back at the truck. She knew that the equipment they had was going to shit. Hell, she'd had to pay for most of the things she'd used on her own desk because there had been no money. She nodded at him, and they entered the very nice restaurant.

~~~

Khan glanced at his brother as the man and woman came across the room toward them. Sebastian had met the man and Khan had only spoken to him. Marvin seemed to be a good man and had been very pissed when he'd figured out that a new hire had been left on his own.

He stood up, realizing that maybe this person was the tech that was left on her own. "I thought you said his name was Kenny. She does not look like any Kenny I've ever seen."

"That's because I said her name was Kerry. Kerry Stephens. Do you ever listen to me?" Khan shook his head and put out his hand for the two of them to shake. The girl looked at his hand a long while before she took it.

"This is Kerry, the woman that had been left to finish the job on her own. I can't tell you again how sorry—" Khan lifted his hand and asked them to have a seat. "I spoke to the customer and she said that Kerry had done a fantastic job, and that she was going to get the rest of our services as well. I'm happy to report that even though it could have been very bad, it turned out very well. This time."

Khan nodded. "I'm Khan Bowen and this is my brother Sebastian. He's the one that convinced the family to buy your company and try to make a go of it." He looked at the girl, who seemed more interested in her phone than him. He cleared his throat and she handed the cell to Marvin.

"I've been working for Friendly Cable for ten years, and I've never worked for a better company. What happened today was a mistake, plain and simple." They both glanced over at Marvin when he said "fuck" very quietly. "I'm sure that Russ McCall thought he was doing me a favor by having me do this on my own, and I'm grateful to him for the experience."

Sebastian laughed and Khan had to try really hard to keep from joining him. He wasn't sure how long she'd been practicing that, but it was the biggest pile of bullshit he'd ever heard.

"I see. And right now you'd go right back out there and work alongside this man again?"

She glanced at Marvin and took back her phone. When she stood, so did the three of them. "Look, I know he's a fuck up. When I was a customer service rep, I'd get four or five calls a week on his shitty attitude as well as his work. But you shouldn't let that keep you from buying out this company." She picked up her bag, and he nearly asked her where the hell she was going when she spoke before he could. "I'm...I have to give you my notice as of right now. I'm sorry, but...I'm sorry."

She was out the door before any of them could comment. Khan nodded to Sebastian, and he took off after her. Marvin looked like someone had hit him between the eyes with a large two-by-four as they both sat down.

"I don't know...well, I know but I don't understand." Marvin looked at him. "She's the only person that's kept us floating for the last six months. Her sales have been nearly three quarters of what everyone else in the office sells. Her family...she has had to deal with her family for all of her life and they are getting worse all the time, and now she's gone."

"Her family? What is it they are doing to her that she'd need to quit this job? I thought...it was my understanding that she loved working for you."

"She does, and I'm sure that hasn't changed, but...." Marvin looked to the front of the restaurant when the door opened and the shouting started. "You'll understand in a moment, I'm sure."

The older man was simply standing there. Khan's first thought was that he looked like a beaten dog with his tail between his legs. But the woman and the younger man standing there had his full attention when he realized that Sebastian was holding the woman back as they both tried to get to Kerry. He stood up and went to them and whistled. All of them stopped shouting and looked at him.

"What the hell is going on here?" He flushed when he realized the entire restaurant was staring at them. "Let's take this to my office, where we can get this settled."

"She won't fucking give me any money to pay the rent." Khan looked at Kerry and back at the screaming woman. "She's selfish and mean, and I don't understand why she just doesn't give it to me."

Kerry said nothing but glared at the older man. It was then that Khan saw the resemblance between the nameless woman and the older man. They were definitely related, and he'd bet that Kerry was a stepsister and that she'd gotten all her looks from the other side of the family. When Sebastian jerked the man back again, Khan stepped in front of Kerry and growled low. His cat wanted blood for her. The younger man was a wolf but nothing compared to Khan, being the head of his family.

"Step back." The wolf sneered at him, and Khan took a step toward him and repeated his command. "I said to step the fuck back from her, or so help me they'll be picking you out of the wallpaper for months, if not years."

"She's going to behave or else." Khan looked back at Kerry, who looked ready to kill them all. He started to take another step toward the man when she turned on her heel and left. Idiot, as he would forever call him—who had actually threatened him—went after her.

Khan wasn't sure what happened in the few seconds it took him to follow them. He was reasonably sure that Kerry—his new best friend—had tried her best to get away from Idiot. But he'd not been smart enough, nor did it appear strong enough, to do battle with her. Kerry was standing over Idiot and he was crying like a small child.

"Kerry?" She turned on him with her fists up, and he took a step back and raised his own hands. "I'm not going to hurt you. I swear it."

She seemed to come back to herself and staggered slightly. He reached for her, almost afraid to, when she collapsed in his arms. He picked her up just as the rest of her family came out of the door.

"Oh, fucking great. Now she'll miss more work and not have enough money to pay my utilities either."

He looked at the other woman, then at Marvin. "Who the hell are these people?" Marvin looked at them as if he, too, wanted to kill them, and nodded to the older man. "This is her father, Norman Stephens. This...person...is her sister—step-sister really—Dora Stephens." He looked down at the man still crying on the drive. "And that miserable excuse for human flesh is Gilbert Baker. He wants everyone to call him Death."

Sebastian didn't even try to stop the laughter that spilled from his mouth. He looked at Khan and they both shook their heads. Their limo pulled up beside them, narrowly missing Death as Khan turned to Marvin again.

"Get in." He nodded and stepped forward. When Dora started to move into the stopped vehicle, her face alight with greed, Sebastian stepped in front of her while Khan got into the car with Kerry. As soon as he was seated, Sebastian got in as well.

"Well, that was a blast." Khan nodded and looked down at the woman in his arms. He didn't have a clue but felt very...well, fuck, protective of her. Marvin cleared his throat and he looked at him.

"Panther?" Both he and Sebastian nodded. "I thought so earlier, but with all the other things going on.... She doesn't know. I'm sure she thinks there is something more to me than simply being her boss, but.... I think she has a little heat exhaustion, as well as more than likely being hungry. She missed her lunch."

"Her family. What the fuck was that all about?" He felt his mate touch his mind and asked her to wait a moment. She laughed. "And what kind of text did she get that made her quit her job just now?"

"They...they're demanding and sucking her dry, if you want to know the truth. They would take her last penny and ask her when she could give them more. It's mostly her father's fault that Dora is like she is. He made Kerry give in to her every whim when they were children, and it hasn't changed much since they are adults. Norman seems to think that he has no control over his little girl, and when Kerry doesn't comply with what they want, Death comes around and knocks her around. He's gotten really good at it over the years." He looked at Kerry as he continued. "They said they were going to visit her at each site she was on and make her lose her job, because they knew she liked it so much. They would too. I had to call the police when they started picketing outside the office last year. She'd refused to give them a credit card where she would pay the bills."

Khan told the driver to take them to his home. He looked at Sebastian and told him to find out what he could, and Sebastian nodded and pulled out his phone. Christ, this was a cluster fuck. Khan told Marvin they were going to have a long conversation when they got to his home, then nodded, sat back, and reached for Monica.

I'm bringing home a woman and a man. Could you have a bedroom set up for her and add them both to the table tonight? There's a mess with the cable company. Her laughter warmed him. *Please?*

Am I to assume that you're not bringing them home for a kinky sex thing? Because if you are, then I'm going to have to decline. You're too much sometimes…I can't think what you'd…. She paused, and he felt her rumble through his mind. *I see. Shall I call in the rest of the family to see what we're going to do about protecting her?*

I don't know. I can't…it's like she needs me and I need to keep her safe. I've never felt this way about a human before, but there is something very…I'm just not sure what it is. You'll have to read her when I get her there.

I will. He felt her cat roar at him. *You should know that I think you're very sweet, but you're going to piss off my cat when you get here. Holding her like you are, and I've not even seen the two of you, makes her crawl all over me.*

I'm sorry, love, I truly am, but she fainted in my arms. What was I supposed to do? He realized that Sebastian was still on the phone with someone and they were nearly home. *I understand she's missed her lunch, and could be dehydrated as well.*

After she told him she'd make sure things were taken care of, they came to a slow, smooth stop in front of the house. As soon as the door was opened to the limo, he saw his dad and Monica come out. This was going to be bad.

CHAPTER 3

Her nose tickled, and she rubbed at it and felt something warm and very soft touch her. Before she could lash out at anyone, she opened her eyes and looked into the most beautiful pair of dark ones she'd ever seen. The little boy had a feather in his hand.

"My uncle gived it to me." She nodded. "Aunt Monica said not to touch you. I didn't."

Kerry was pretty sure that he had but didn't comment about that. "Do I know you? And do you know where I am?"

"Bed. I can't tell you my name is George on accounta Momma said I can't be a good boy if I do." She nodded and tried to keep from smiling at him. "You can tell me your name. Then I can tell you."

"Kerry Stephens." She sat up just as the door opened. The little body nearly took her out when he moved so quickly off the bed to stand next to it. He looked at the woman in the doorway as if she was already yelling at him.

"George Bowen, what did I tell you about coming in here?" He looked at her and then back at the woman. "George?"

"You said not to come in here and detrub her. You said she needed her nap time." He glanced at her again. "Aunt Monica, I didn't touch her like you said."

She walked over to the bed and pulled the spread back. There on the pristine cover was a small shoe print. Kerry watched the little boy as he tried to think how to get out of this one, because Kerry had no doubt that this wasn't the first time he'd been in trouble, and she'd bet her next commission check it wasn't even the first time today. She stood up and had to reach for the post at the head of the bed.

"Khan said you'd missed your lunch, as well as were low on fluids. If you think you can make it, I'll have the cook fix you something light for now. The rest of them are in the study." She moved toward her. "I'm Monica Bowen and this is George, our nephew. How are you feeling?"

She nodded that she was fine but didn't let go of the post just yet. "How did I get here? And where is here?"

"Khan, my husband, brought you, and this is our home. You fainted when you were having a meeting with him and my brother-in-law, Sebastian. Something about the new cable company we're going to buy." Kerry nodded and let go of the bed. "You need some help?"

"No. If you could figure out a way for me to get back to my job site, I'd appreciate it. This is my first day on the job and I'm pretty sure I might be in trouble." She tried to smile, but she just wasn't feeling it. Who took a stranger to their home and put them in one of their beds?

"You'd be surprised." Kerry looked at the woman, then at the little boy who pulled on her shirt. He smiled up at her, and she smiled back.

"You should meet my grandpa. He's an old prink." Kerry looked at Monica, who moaned. "Mommy calls him that all the time, and so does Aunt Monica."

He'd stretched out the word *all* so that she knew that he had heard that numerous times. She also suspected that he wasn't an old "prink" but an old "prick." She laughed when Monica told George to go to the kitchen and tell cook to fix a light snack for her and him.

"I'm not staying. I have to get back. I have things to finish up." At least she hoped that she did. "I thank you for letting me rest here, but I have to get back. Now. Today."

"You work for the cable company, right? I understand that you were left on a job alone and yet you finished it completely, even with it being only your first day." Kerry shook her head. "You didn't finish it?"

"I did, but it's not my first day. I've worked for the company for a long time. It was just my first day as a lineman. And I'd very much like it not to be my last." Kerry moved toward the door and the woman. "Thank you again."

Kerry wasn't sure she'd let her pass, and when she did, the woman leaned in and sniffed her. It made all the hair on her arms dance, and she took a step back before she did something again, like bite her. Monica smiled and followed her down the stairs, and nodded to the right when she looked back for directions.

To say the kitchen was huge would have been a major understatement. And it was crowded as well. Although there were only five people in the room, they were large and muscular, which made Kerry nervous. She took a step back and bumped into someone when one of them seemed to lunge toward her. She stood with her back to the refrigerator as the man behind her stepped away.

The man in front of her stopped and smiled. "I'm sorry. You're slightly overwhelmed right now. I'm Dylan, Dylan Bowen. You're Kerry Stephens. Little George told us you were coming down." She didn't take the hand he held out, somehow getting the feeling that if he touched her then she'd be...she wasn't sure what would happen, but she kept her hands to herself.

"I was just going to call a cab." She looked at the phone across the room. It seemed miles away across dangerous grounds. She had no idea where that thought came from, but she was sure she wasn't far off the mark. She looked at the older man who came in from the outside. He looked like these men, only older. He nodded to her and told the others to back off.

"Can't you see you're scaring the piss out of her? Bunch of morons." An older woman came in the door behind him and he turned to her. "They're ganging up on her and she's ready to bolt. Can see it in her eyes."

Kerry looked at the woman and felt she'd seen her before. When it occurred to her, she let out a long breath, not even realizing that she'd been holding it. The woman smiled at her when Kerry smiled first.

"I remember you. We shared a table the other morning at that place on Seventh." She nodded. "You told me your name was...Corrine."

"Yes. Who would have thought we'd see each other again?" She opened the refrigerator and took out a large pitcher. "Come and have a seat, dear. I'll have someone take you home after you've had a bite to eat. And something to drink. I think we're having steaks on the grill tonight. I'm sure Khan and Monica won't mind if you join us."

"No, we'd love you to come; please do." Monica handed her a plate with a thick roast beef sandwich on it, as well as a sliced up apple. "We'll all be here, so it will be even more overwhelming than it is now. There are a total of thirteen of us coming. Reed and Caitlynne just returned from DC, and we've been planning this for a month."

Kerry took a bite of the half sandwich she'd picked up. It was delicious. She moaned and looked at Monica as she chewed. When George sat next to her she offered him the apple slices. She didn't care for them.

"I'm sorry, but I can't. I have to work tomorrow and I have no car here." She didn't even know if she could get her car now, because she had parked it near the truck she was out in today on the lot. "I need to get going. Thanks."

"I insist." She looked up at Khan, the man she'd seen earlier. "You're going to stay for dinner, then we'll talk about this business with the man who left you on your own today. He needs to be punished for what he did. How many other times has he—?"

She stood up and he shut up. There was something very...wonderful about having a man as large as him backing away from her. When she reached for the other half of the sandwich and wrapped it in her napkin, no one spoke. But as she made her way to the door Khan stepped in front of her and she snapped.

"What the fuck do you think you're doing? I'm not sure what decade you live in, but in this one it's considered bad form to bring someone to your home without their permission, and it's kidnapping if you don't let them leave." She heard the older man laugh and decided she liked him. "I said I want to go, and you'll either let me or so help me I'll knock you on your ass."

The door behind her opened again but she didn't turn. She was afraid it was another man and she had enough going on with the one in front of her. When he smiled at her she frowned. She'd never been aggressive to a stranger before, but it had worked on Death pretty good when she'd confronted him over the weekend.

"Khan, what's going on here?" The newcomer. She had no idea why she knew that, but she turned just a little to look at him and nearly moaned.

The other men were good looking, handsome as a matter of fact, with dark hair as well as dark eyes, but this man was...more. He had the same dark good looks, but he didn't seem to overwhelm her. As a matter of fact, she wanted to snuggle up to him and let him hold her. She turned away from him, embarrassed at where her mind had gone. But when he came up behind her and put his hands on her shoulders, she stiffened, suddenly terrified.

"This is Kerry Stephens. She is going to work with us on the cable project. I'm sure with her experience she can...."

Khan stopped talking and she opened her eyes, not even realizing that she'd closed them. The warm breath on her bare neck made her dizzy.

She heard chairs scrape and thought someone growled. She wasn't sure about the second thing, and decided that she didn't hear the man holding her do that. Before she could tell him to let her go, Khan nodded once and stepped from in front of her. The door closed and she was turned around.

~~~

Reed looked at her but didn't let her go. She was beautiful even with the sunburn on her nose and forehead. He wanted to take her hair down and see if it was as soft as it looked, but didn't want to let go of her just yet. When she took a step back from him he growled again. She looked at him oddly.

"Is there something wrong with you?" He shook his head. "The reason I'm asking is because you're holding onto me like I'm holding you up, and you seem to be under the impression that growling at me is okay. It's not, in case you're wondering."

"I'm Reed Bowen." She didn't say anything and he found that he wasn't sure what to do. "I'm just coming home from DC. I've been working and living there for about three years now."

"Good for you. Let me go." He did so reluctantly. "Thank you. Now if you don't mind, I'd like to leave. It's been really...I started to say nice, but this is the strangest family I've ever seen. And now I must go."

"No." She looked at him again, and this time he could see she wasn't happy with him. "I mean, I'd rather you didn't. I want to get to know you."

She didn't say anything but moved toward the door. He followed her, and when she put her hand on the knob he pulled her body to his so that he was spooned behind her. Reed leaned into her throat again and licked along the long column of it. She trembled under his touch and he bit gently at her flesh.

"Don't do that again." Her voice was husky, warm feeling, and he wanted more than anything to turn her around and press her against the door so he could kiss her, but he couldn't let her go just yet, even to do that.

"Don't leave me." He licked again, taking as much of her taste into his mouth as he could. "I want you to come home with me...no, that won't work. I don't have a bed yet. But we could go to a hotel." Before he could clarify what he'd meant to say, he felt his body fall backwards and then nothing else.

~~~

Reed looked up at Khan and Marc, wondering why they were looking down him and not standing in front of him. He had no idea what was going on, but he was soaking wet and they were laughing hard. He started to sit up when a boot on his chest held him there.

"Not yet, little brother. Walker went to get his bag. You might have a concussion." Reed frowned at Sebastian. "She really hit you hard."

"Who did?" He looked around the room for Kerry and then at his brothers. "Where is she? What did you do with her?"

Khan laughed. "Dad took her home. She didn't look all that thrilled to be here once she knocked you on your ass. What did she use anyway? The chair?"

"I don't...what the hell happened here, and why the fuck is Dad taking her home? I told her I was...."

He tried to remember what had happened. He'd told her about his bed, then he'd mentioned a hotel. He looked up at Kahn, who nodded at him as if to say he was glad he got it.

"She hit me." His brothers laughed. "What the hell did she do that for? She's my mate, for Christ's sake. I wasn't going to hurt her."

"But you didn't tell her that, and even if you did, it's doubtful she would have understood." His mom hit him in the head when he was helped up and sat in a chair. "You idiot. What the blazes were you thinking treating her that way?"

"I didn't do anything to her." But he had, now that he thought about it. He'd treated her badly, suggesting they go to a hotel, and they'd not even as much as kissed. "I was a bastard. And I should have known better than to treat her the way I did."

Walker looked him over and told him that he'd been lucky he'd only hit the table on his way down and not the stove. It was metal and he might have bent it. As it was the table was broken. For some idiotic reason Reed was proud of her for knocking him out. When everyone left but his mom and Monica, he looked at them sheepishly.

"I found her and scared her off." Monica nodded. "I didn't think about...I guess I didn't think at all. But she was right here and I couldn't help but want to mark her."

"And now she's gone." His mom patted his hand and stood up. "What do you plan to do about all this? Are you going to stalk her again and make her even more terrified of you? I don't think she'll go very easily."

Reed didn't have a clue what to do. He wanted her to be his mate, have the same relationship that his brothers had with theirs, but he didn't want to have all the turmoil that they'd had leading up to it. He looked around the room and saw something just under the cabinet. He stood up to get it and nearly fell over. She'd hit him pretty hard. Monica leaned over and picked it up for him.

"What is this?" Reed turned it over in his hands twice before he realized it was some sort of drive. He'd seen this sort of thumb drive in the stores a lot lately, different character shapes that had a drive as part of their inner workings. This one was a small white dog with a little yellow bird on his shoulder. He took it to his nose and sneezed when he smelled it.

"She's touched this, but there is also wolf on it. Her scent is stronger because its fresh, but I would bet that this belongs to the wolf." Reed looked up at Monica and his mom. "I don't think he likes her overly much either."

He wanted to take it and put it into a computer to find out what was on it. He knew for some reason it wasn't going to be a good thing, and looked up when his brothers came back in. This time they were very serious as he told them what he'd found.

"You think it's hers?" He nodded at Marc. "Well, I wouldn't just put it into a computer without having something secure attached to it. There's no telling what could be on it, or once it's in the system what it could do if connected to a network. Would you like for me to have a look?"

"I can do it, but just in case there is something on it I'd very much like for you to be there. It might be nothing more than a few pictures, but I don't think so, do you?" Marc shook his head. "I have a laptop here if you think that'll do it. We'll take off the wireless and make sure it's dead to the rest of them before we start."

He went out to the car to get his computer and thought about the woman. He wanted to go and find her now, but knew that if he did she'd more than likely hit him again. Smiling, he wondered what she would taste like when he got her to let him mark her. He adjusted his cock as it hardened and told him to behave. He was going to have to work on making her trust him before he could think of her under him. He felt his cock stir again and his cat race along his skin, begging him to go and find her.

"Later buddy. I promise." He grinned bigger. "And when we do have her where we want her, we'll make sure we can keep her there. I'm thinking we'll keep her sated. That way she won't have the strength to leave."

He was still smiling when he entered the house. Reed knew he was only twenty five, but he was ready to settle down with his mate. More than he'd thought possible.

CHAPTER 4

Kerry knew it was too much to hope that the Bowens wouldn't be in the office the next morning when she got there. Five people had told her that the new owners had come in the three very large limos that sat out in the front of the building. Marvin had told her last night after she'd gotten home that they'd bought the cable company. And that both Robbie and Russ had been terminated.

"He, that bigger man, said that he'd not have the type of problems that occurred with you again. He seemed to think you've had issues with Robbie before and asked me about them. I had to tell him love, I'm sorry."

"Not to worry. It was bound to come out anyway." She had already been told that the Bowens were interviewing everyone about the working conditions, and wanted to know what was needed to improve things. "A couple of people told me that they'd told them about Robbie and Russ anyway."

"They were a pain in the ass to a great many people. I'm just hoping the new owners keep this up with weeding out the bad." Marvin laughed. "Well, okay, not too many of the bad weeds. We do need people to answer the phone. Not to change the subject too quickly here, but how are you feeling from yesterday? Did you finally get something to eat?"

"Yeah, and a good night's sleep too. Amazing what a few hours of exhausted sleep will do for a person." She smiled at him. "And a thick hamburger with all the trimmings, large order of fries, and three glasses of water. Thanks for the loan until payday."

He waved her off. "When you fainted I nearly joined you. I should have made sure you had plenty to drink before I put you in there with them. And that's another thing. Mr. Bowen is making sure that everyone has a way to communicate with the offices. He said that we should have had that all along. I told him that you'd said so too on many occasions, even as a CSR. I started to explain to him that a CSR is a customer service representative, but he knew already. I like the man."

She'd told him last night about being taken to his house, but left out the part where she'd been licked by one of his brothers. She was still trying to wrap her mind around that one. And then there was the small bite mark on her shoulder she'd found this morning after her shower, where she just knew that man had bitten her.

Kerry was just clocking in when she heard her name being called. She turned to look at another problem she had. This one woman was ten times worse than Robbie had ever been. She started to smile at her but thought *Fuck it, I don't answer to her any longer.*

"They want you in the big office." Kerry didn't ask who but Agnes seemed to be on a mission to tell her. "There are six men and five women in there that look like they stepped out of some rich and famous magazine. I think they want to fire you. Be a blessing if they did. You're a pain in the ass."

"I doubt it. They would have told me yesterday when I was at their house if that was the plan." She walked away from Agnes, smiling. That was fun. Childish, but extremely fun.

They were all there, and as she was walking in the elder Mr. and Mrs. Bowen were shown in as well. Marvin stepped forward and she could see the strain on his face. They had upset him, and she looked at Khan.

"You have no right to make this man feel upset like this for no reason whatsoever. He's been running this company for nearly a year without much in the way of support from anyone. If you want to be pissy to someone, be that way to the previous owners, who took all our retirement money as well as all the extra equipment with them when they skipped the country." Khan raised a brow at her but she was on a roll. "And what the hell did you come in here full force for? You trying to make the rest of the people here feel afraid? Or is that your plan, to intimidate them enough that they quit? I think you're going to have your work cut out for you on that score. There hasn't ever been a more lazy bunch of supervisors working anywhere than the ones here, and they haven't a clue how this place runs. And they bark and bite all the time. The CSR's will make or break you."

She looked at Reed when she realized what she'd said about biting. She felt the one at her shoulder tingle when he looked back at her. There was something both terrifying and sexy about the way he was staring at her, like she was a Thanksgiving meal and Christmas gifts all in one. She shivered as she turned to Khan again.

"Are you finished?" She flushed when he asked her. "We came in here together so that we could all look the company over. Walker is a doctor, so you'll see the least of him. Dylan is a teacher, but will come in from time to time to have a look at some of the rules and make sure they're up to date. He's going to be the head of our human resources department. Marc here has a great deal of experience in other fields, such as investigative work, and will assist Dylan when necessary. Sebastian, as well as Reed, have a great deal of knowledge about computers, and are going to see about getting the ones here updated to something in this century. My parents are here because they, for whatever reason, like you."

"And you?" He grinned at her and she had a feeling that he was here because he was head honcho. "What do you think you can contribute to this company besides the money and being bossy?"

"I *am* the boss." He pointed to the chair that was next to Reed and asked her to sit. She really didn't have a choice and they both knew it. She needed this job until she found something else. And she was going to start looking as soon as she had a break.

"These are the orders taken over the phone for the past ninety days." She took the papers that Dylan had given her. "I've taken the names off to protect the others, but not yours. Can you tell me why you transferred to be a line person and didn't stay at the phones? You're very good, as you know. And the best person we have on staff to encourage and get upgrades."

"It's lineman, not person. And you met Robbie I take it?" He nodded. "Then you know. Besides, I love being out of doors no matter the weather. I've been working at the same desk for more years than most people stay married. I needed a change."

He nodded. "You're the best this company has. Your sales alone count for over three quarters of what all the others sell. And that's not all. You handle issues that come up well, too. You've been able to save more customers than the others because you're extremely good at calming the situation and making the customer feel good about the fact that you've had to shut him off."

She was embarrassed. Kerry squirmed in her seat and her breath caught when a hand landed on her knee. She looked at Reed and he moved it back, slowly running his fingers up her thigh to her hip. Her body burned for more but she turned away, not understanding this at all.

Kerry looked at Mr. Bowen and had a feeling he knew what his son had just done to her. She looked at Sebastian, who stood up to turn on a computer. She was surprised to see his screen shining on the wall behind him. The cables in this office hadn't worked since she'd been there.

"Here is a list of all the people who work here. Most of them are doing well, but we feel they can improve with a bit more training." He looked at her. "I don't think they've had much more training than a few sheets of paper handed to them, have they?"

"There used to be a training program when I first started here. It would help new hires to get the terminology down, as well as how to reference anything you needed off the system. But the system hasn't been updated in the past five years, and the trainer was promoted to something over her head and was fired shortly after. I think she works for your competitor in another state." She felt Reed's heat when he moved his leg closer to her, and she tried to think what she'd been saying. "I have my old training manuals if you want them. They're mostly outdated, but I try to keep up with them. I used to make copies for anyone that wanted them, but quit that when I was written up. I couldn't prove I'd paid for the copies out of my own pocket, and no matter how many receipts I brought in, it didn't seem to matter. I don't do it now."

Sebastian nodded. "I'd like to have them if you don't mind. And would you mind going over them with me? When you bring them in, we'll figure out what we need to update and what no longer applies."

Kerry nodded. "They're in my car. I'd planned to give them to you anyway. I've no real use for them anymore. I also have the manuals that I was given the other day to look at for the lineman position. I wondered, do I still have the job?"

"Why on earth would you think otherwise?" She looked at Khan when he answered her. "Christ woman, I can't run this company without you. You've single handedly kept this company afloat. I'm hoping you'll continue."

When she stood to go and get the manuals, all of them stood as well. She looked at Mrs. Bowen, wondering if she was the one who'd taught them to stand when a woman did. It seemed old fashioned, but they were all a little on the weird side. When she went out the door she hadn't realized that Reed had come with her until he opened the outer door for her.

"I can do this by myself. Why don't you go in there and wait for me?" He just smiled at her and she wanted to punch him in his very beautiful lips...mouth. She turned and left him standing there to go to her car, and nearly screamed when she turned around and he was right in front of her.

"I'd very much like to kiss you." She shook her head at his request. "Why not? Are you afraid of me, Kerry?"

His voice was low, and she thought if it were something real she could feel it touch her skin. When she shook her head again at him he leaned closer to her and she licked her lips.

"Do you have any idea what it does to me to have you sitting so close to me and not be able to do all the things I want to?" She didn't know what he meant, so didn't answer him. "Let me kiss you, please. I'll try to behave for the rest of the meeting if you do."

He wasn't going to behave anytime, and she had no idea why she knew that. As his head lowered to hers she licked her lips again, wanting to beg him to please hurry. When his warm mouth brushed over hers gently, she felt her knees weaken. He put his hand on her hip and held her as he ran his tongue over her suddenly dry lips.

"Let me in, Kerry. Let me taste paradise." She moaned when he nipped at her lower lip then suckled it into his mouth. When he let it go she could almost taste him, and wanted more. He cupped the back of her head and brought her to him.

Christ, he didn't just kiss her, but took her. His mouth, his tongue danced along hers as if he was devouring her. When his body pressed against hers she put her hands on his waist to hold on, because he was making her weak.

Reed tore his mouth from hers and looked down at her. His eyes had darkened and she could see something deep within them. A beast was all she could think of, but before she could be afraid he was kissing her again. She nearly cried out when he rocked into her soft folds.

Her body wasn't just hot but flaming out of control, and he was the accelerant. Moaning against his mouth when he cupped her ass and brought her closer to him, she moved her arms up to his neck to hold on, she told herself. What she really wanted was for him to tear her clothes off and take her right then. As his mouth moved from hers to her neck, then to the sensitive place behind her ear, she felt his teeth nip at her again.

He was going to mark her and she felt her body react to the thought. She wanted him to sink his teeth into her hard, and wondered for a brief second where that thought had come from when he whispered for her to come. He rocked hard into her again and again, and she couldn't stop her body from reacting even if she'd wanted to.

She cried out her release. It was quick, hard, and not nearly satisfying enough. When he commanded her to come again, she felt his teeth graze her throat and knew that he was going to do it. He was going to bite her. When his teeth sank deep she screamed out a release so powerful that she felt explosions and saw stars behind her closed eyes. Then everything went black.

~~~

Reed held her to his body as he realized what they'd done. What he'd done. He'd marked her. Not that he didn't want to take her, but he'd hoped to do so without it being against her car in a very public place. He looked around, glad that she'd parked in this lot and that no one was around. He picked her up in his arms and held her while he reached for his brother.

I'm here with her and she's...I think she's fainted. He couldn't help but grin at that. *I'm...I've claimed her, marked her. She's...Christ, Khan, all I can think about is taking her home and finishing what we've started.*

Damn it Reed. He felt his brother's anger but it was soon replaced with a great deal of humor. *She's going to fucking kill you when she wakes up. Bring her in here so we can all watch.*

I'm not...what the fuck, Khan? I tell you I have a mate and you want to watch her be upset with me because I've done it? What is wrong with you? His brother laughed through their connection. *I'm not bringing her in unless you promise to behave.*

Oh, I'll behave all right. And if you think she's only going to be upset, then you're nuts. She's going to be fucking pissed, and you know it as well as I do.

Kerry started to stir in his arms and he closed the connection to his brother. All he was doing was laughing anyway, so there was no point in continuing. When she opened her eyes she smiled at him and he let out a breath. She wasn't mad. But her fist connected with his nose so quickly that he nearly dropped her.

"What the hell was that?" He watched her nearly leap from his arms, and backed up when she took a few steps toward him.

"Did we just have sex? Out here? In the fucking parking lot?"

"Technically we didn't have sex. You came. And quite beautifully too." He took another step back when she advanced on him again. "Now Kerry, there's no reason to get upset. I'm still hard as a rock and you're supposed to be relaxed. Didn't you enjoy that?"

She opened her mouth to say something, and then put her hand over the small scar at her throat. He felt his cock harden more when he thought of biting her again. But the look on her face made him think that if he tried she really would kill him.

"You monster." He looked behind him, knowing she couldn't be talking about him. "You're a sick son of a bitch, and…and I want you to stay away from me. From now on."

"You work for me, and as of now you and I are…we're a couple. I can't let you go and you won't want me to. I need you to—" He took another step back when she doubled up her fist again. "Do you always react so violently when you're pissed off?"

"As a matter of fact no, you just bring out the worst in me." She started toward the building then turned. He thought she was coming to him, but she went to her car, pulled out a large tote, and went to the building again. He decided when she went inside without a backward glance that he might have handled this better. He followed her inside but at a great distance. He thought to give her time to cool off.

He was standing in the call center, the large area where the phones were being answered, when he heard a shout. He turned to the door in time to see Kerry coming out, followed closely by his father. He looked as mad as he'd ever seen him. What had she done now?

"I didn't mean to make you upset, Kerry, but it's as plain as the nose on your face that he's done something else to you." His dad looked at him when he saw him. "Tell her. Tell her that she's better off coming with us to stay than going home where she's not safe."

"Where is it?" He looked at his dad then at her when she put out her hand and repeated herself. "I want it right now. You had no right to look on that in the first place. It wasn't...it's mine and you'll give it back to me."

It took him several seconds to realize what she was talking about. The thumb drive. He started to nod to her when Marc came out of the office and shook his head. Reed looked at Kerry.

"Do you know what's on there?" She flushed and he knew that she did. "Did you give him permission to take those pictures or did he do this all on his own?"

"I'm not going to justify that with an answer. You acting like you're any better than him after what happened out there is ludicrous. Give me the drive." He glanced at his brother then looked at her.

"Is he blackmailing you?" She simply stared at him but he could feel her fear. "If so then I can take care of him for you. You're my mate and it's my duty to make sure that—"

"I have no idea what you're talking about, but it's really a moot point since we're nothing to each other." She looked over her shoulder at the others, and he could see her embarrassment when she looked at him. "They've seen them too, haven't they?"

"Only Marc and I have, but the others know." He watched her face pale and stepped forward to hold her, but she stopped him by taking a step back. "Is he blackmailing you?"

Her eyes filled with tears and his heart hurt. Reed wanted to take her home and hold her; he wanted to keep her from hurting as much he was sure she was right now. When she handed the bag that she'd taken out of her car to Khan, he thought she'd talk to them about all of this, but she nodded once and wiped at the tears.

"I quit."

She was out the door before his family could react. He was right behind her when she got to her car and jerked her around to tell her she was being stupid. But a noise to his right had him turning and pushing her away at the same time she jerked his arm. He was suddenly in front of her car when something, a large flash of fur, leapt at them. He didn't know what the hell happened, but his head exploded in pain. The last thing he saw was her being knocked to the ground by a large panther. Khan had saved her.

CHAPTER 5

Khan watched his brother rest. He wasn't happy with Kerry any more than he was his brother right now, but she wasn't here and Reed was. He wanted to reach out and shake the shit out of him, but knew that he'd hit his head and Walker said he had to rest. His mom walked in just as he was contemplating doing what he wanted.

"What have you done about the people who saw you?" He looked at her, then back at his brother. "It's already on the news that a large panther is on the loose. They have a manhunt out for him."

"Well, they can look all they want, but I doubt very much they'll come here asking us about it."

"Do not be a smart ass, young man. I'm still your mother and I will be respected. I've asked you a simple question and a simple answer is what you'll give me." She tapped her foot as she waited, a sure sign that she was not happy. "Well?"

"I'm sorry. I'm just...Christ. That wolf was going for her throat, and had I waited to make sure that there was no one around, then she'd be dead and we both know it."

"I know but...will he be all right?" He told her what Walker had told him about a nasty bump on his head and the wound that had already sealed up. "She tossed him behind her to save him. I never...she threw him over the car, Khan. What do you suppose that means for her, for them?"

"I'm not sure." He thought of the things she'd said to his dad when he'd taken her into his arms. "She said that she could smell him. That his name was Death or something like that; she was hysterical. Do you think it's the same wolf that took those pictures?"

The pictures. He'd finally gotten to see some of them when he'd tracked down Sebastian. Someone had taken a great many pictures of Kerry while she'd been in her home. All of them of her nude, and some of those very close up. He glanced at his mom when she cleared her throat.

"What are we going to do about this person, Khan? You know that he's not going to stop now. He proved that today." He knew. The man had tried to kill her. And Khan had a feeling that he wasn't blackmailing her like they'd thought. At least not for money, but for something bigger, and more than likely more than the girl could afford to give up.

"Has Monica looked to see what she is?" He looked at Reed, who was struggling to sit up when he spoke. He went to the bed to help him, suddenly feeling horrible about his thoughts from earlier. He didn't know what he'd do if something happened to his family. He loved them more than he could ever tell anyone.

"No. The girl hasn't touched a great many of us. I think she has some sort of clue what could happen if she does." He sat back down and their mom left the room to get Reed something to eat. "You're her mate now. Do you have any idea what she is?"

"No." Reed sat on the edge of the bed with his head down. "I've really fucked this up. And I was going to have the best mating ever. I've been taking notes on things not to do to mine, and here I fucked it up anyway. I guess she's gone."

"Yes. Right after Walker said you were going to make it, she took off. I didn't think to have her stay with us, but...." He looked around the room, thinking again of Reed going over that car. "She's not wholly human. And she saved your ass."

"And you saved her. I thank you for that." Reed stood up and went to the bathroom. Khan waited, knowing that Reed would need to find out some things about her, about his mate and the wolf that Khan had tangled with. Not to mention what Marc and Sebastian had uncovered about Kerry.

When he came out he looked better and sat in the chair across from him. "Tell me. I can see on your face that you know something. Just tell me."

"The wolf from today is probably the same one that had the thumb drive. I'm not sure that he took the pictures, but she...she was babbling after I took off after the wolf, and Dad said she'd tried to make him understand things were fine. But she said that Death—and I'm not sure yet if that's a name or something like a reference to a man—but someone had sicced a wild animal on her before. She told Dad that there was no such thing as shifters. Dad said she brought up the word shifters, not him."

"You think she's had an encounter with one before and can't wrap her mind around it?" Khan nodded. "What happened today? Do you...I think she saved me from being attacked. Did she?"

"Yes. She threw you over the car and out of the way of the wolf that attacked her. A few seconds, and I mean just a few seconds, more and you would have been torn apart before you could have shifted. When he went for her throat after you were out, I...I've had this need to protect her even before I knew she was your mate. I'm not sure what it is about her but...." Khan looked at the window before he could continue. "I've seen the pictures and saw the marks on her. Do you suppose she's protecting someone, and whoever took the pictures wanted them?"

"I honestly don't know. But I've been...we've found she has a sister and a father still that live around here. I don't have a great deal of information about them, but I'm digging. Her mother, for some reason, isn't coming up anywhere on anything. Not even her birth certificate. It simply says unknown. The man listed as her father is the one that she has down as next of kin in the event of an emergency, but...." Khan looked at Reed as he seemed to think about what else he wanted to say. "I'd be dead before I called him in to help me. He's not a good man and seems to be somewhat of a drunk. And that's just the stuff I pulled off the police record that I had run."

"Somewhat of a drunk? What does that mean?"

Reed shrugged and looked at the door when little George came in and stared at them both. "Hey buddy."

It was all the invitation he needed to come in and leap at his uncle. Reed held him close to him as he stood up and they all walked into the hall together. George was talking a mile a minute about anything and nothing. Reed seemed to know just what he was talking about too. Khan couldn't wait for his children to do more than string words together without it making a great deal of sense.

"Okay, I'll see what I can do about it. But she's kind of mad at me right now and I have to think of ways to tell her I'm sorry." Khan watched George stare at him. The kid was pretty smart and cocked his brow at him.

"Can't you make her come here, Uncle Khan? Mommy says that you think you're the boss. Make Kerry come back and play with me."

He decided to ignore the part where his mom thought he was in charge and answer the little guy. He'd take care of Caitlynne later...maybe. She was one scary assed woman. "I can't make her, George. Kerry has to want to come here and be with us." Khan looked up at his brother. "I think she might come back if Uncle Reed here tells her how sorry he is for making her pi...mad at him."

"You go call her now and tell her," George told Reed. "She's a nice lady and I want her to come back and play with me."

Khan watched as Reed tried not to laugh. "I want to play with her too, but I think she's really mad at me. I might have to grovel and get down on my hands and knees a great deal before she'll believe me." The double meaning was lost on their nephew, but Khan nearly burst out laughing when Reed winked at him. "I'll see what I can do though, how about that?"

George took off running when they were on the last step. He and his brother walked into the living room just as someone's cell phone went off. Dylan answered it and left the room. Jack, his mate and very pregnant wife, went with him.

When he returned, Dylan was smiling. "I found her. She's got an apartment near downtown. I'm sending some of the pack that helps me over to keep an eye on her and to see if any other wolf has been snooping around."

Khan nodded and looked at Reed as he began pulling his coat on. When he reached for his keys, no one said a word. This was something the two of them had to straighten out, and no matter how much he wanted to go with him to help him, Khan knew that even if they took the next ten years to work out their differences, they'd get there eventually.

~~~

Kerry was just scooping up her second bowl of raspberry sherbet when someone knocked on the door. She put the frozen treat away before making her way to the front of her apartment, knowing that whoever was there now didn't know her. Few people, her family included, knew where she was living now and she wanted to keep it that way. She'd moved out of her old apartment a few weeks ago, just after getting the message in her mail box. She looked out the peep hole and nearly groaned when she saw Marvin there.

She opened the door for him and he started to come in. Kerry watched his face as he looked at her. There was always something very strange about this man. Instead of asking him what it was, she told him to either come in or not, she had ice cream melting. Then she left him there as she made her way back to the kitchen. He showed up just as she was sitting at the table.

"You've been to see one of the Bowens, I see." She had no idea why she had an overwhelming urge to touch the place on her neck, but she resisted, just barely. "Which one was it? The younger one I bet."

He leaned back against her refrigerator while she ate. When she offered him some of her treat he declined. *Just as well*, she thought, *there isn't but a little bit left*. When she finished she put her bowl in the sink and went to the living room.

To call this an apartment was grossly overstating its worth. The area that she used as a bedroom had the tiniest closet she'd ever seen. The bathroom had a single tiny sink plus a stand up shower — which at best one medium sized person would be able to use — and a commode. The shower, when in use, needed to be a quick one because the water chilled rather quickly. The living room, bedroom, and kitchen all shared the same space, and that was barely large enough for a loveseat and a television, no table, and the appliances. One large open room with all the comforts of home. She could lie in her bed and watch the television while cooking her dinner. Life was good.

She sat on her loveseat and waited for Marvin to speak to her.

"You do know that what happened yesterday is not going to go away. Neither you nor I will be able to turn the Bowens away after all of this, nor is you being hurt in the process going to set well with them."

Kerry tried her best not to see that he was right. What had happened still embarrassed her. Kerry didn't think he'd ever seen the pictures of her but wasn't sure. She looked at him when he paused in his praising of the Bowens.

"You seriously don't think I'm going back there, do you? Not that it matters, because they won't want me anyway. I'm pretty sure that I burned that bridge." Marvin leaned back in his chair and stared at her. Kerry picked up the remote. She'd lose her free cable, too, when she lost her job, but she'd figure something out. She wasn't going back.

"They offered you a fat bonus if you came back." She snorted. "I'm telling you the truth, love. That man, Khan, he said he'd make it well worth your while. They lost three more today after that young Dylan took them in his office. One of them was your good friend Agnes. She didn't take it well." Kerry would bet not. "She threatened that young man of yours."

"I don't have a man, young or otherwise." She felt the scar burn and had an overwhelming feeling that she should run. Not away, like she thought she should, but in the direction of the door and the man who'd bitten her. When someone knocked she looked at Marvin, who shrugged at her.

She looked in the peep hole again and groaned. Reed laughed. Stupid man must be able to hear a pin drop. She didn't open the door but stood there while she tried to think what to do. He laughed again.

"You might as well let me in. And the man that's in there with you will need to leave. I don't want to have to hurt him because he's there." She looked at Marvin, who was pulling on his coat.

"You are not leaving." He simply continued to pull on his coat then his gloves. "This is just stupid. Why on earth do you think you have to leave because he said so? It's my home."

He kissed her cheek and they both heard Reed growl. Marvin reached for the door and opened it just as she was ready to protest again. Reed had a large bouquet of the deepest colored red roses she'd ever seen. Her eyes widened when he also handed her a large box of chocolates. The little thumb drive was attached to the bow.

"Little George sent the candy. He said to buy you a bag of suckers, but I liked these better." She took them as he shoved them at her. "The flowers are from me. I nearly didn't get the red ones, but I saw these and couldn't resist. They're beautiful, like you are."

He laid the roses on what she could now see was a ten pound box of chocolates. She looked up at him as he bid Marvin a good night, then stared at him as he stood in the hall.

"What did you do?" He frowned at her. "No man spends his entire check on flowers and candy unless he's done something wrong."

"I hurt you."

She was pretty sure he didn't mean just today when he'd grabbed her. Her arm still hurt, but she thought it was because she'd hurt herself pushing him out of the way. The bruising was still coming on, but she could see his finger prints.

"Can I come in?"

She stepped back and felt the room shrink in size the moment he stepped over the threshold. It hadn't felt this tiny when Marvin had been there with her. Both men were built the same but.... She looked at the roses when she realized she was staring at him.

"Don't take off your coat. You're not staying that long." He did it anyway and laid it over the back of her couch. She went to the kitchen area and put her flowers in the only thing she could find, a large pitcher. She looked up when she heard her bed creak, and started forward to kick him out.

"It's nice and firm. Perfect." She glared at him when he lay back on the bed. "Do you have any aspirin? I have a pounding headache. Walker gave me something for it, but I couldn't take it and drive."

"You expect me to believe that you drove all the way here to borrow an aspirin?" He shook his head and winced. She immediately went to find him something to take.

When she went back to the bed, he was asleep. She started to wake him, not sure if he should be sleeping, and decided to find out. She took out the business card that Sebastian had given her and called the number on it. An answering service answered after the fourth ring.

"My name is Kerry Stephens and I'd like to speak to Mr. Bowen if it's possible please. It's about his brother." She was told to hang on please. When someone answered, she knew it wasn't Sebastian. The woman was laughing.

"Hello, my dear. What have you done, killed him? I probably would have. By the way, I'm Ama. The one with the tats." Kerry didn't think they were tats any more than she thought the woman was Sebastian.

"Mr. Bowen, Reed Bowen, is here and he's come for an aspirin. I'm pretty sure he didn't come all this way for just that, but he did have a box of candy he said was from little George and a...." She hated babblers and she was fast becoming one. "Reed Bowen is here and he's sleeping. Is that all right?"

"Let me ask Walker. He's standing right here." There was a muffled conversation and she decided that she should have simply tossed Reed out on his ass and been done with it. But Doctor Bowen came on the line.

"He can sleep if he wants, but I would very much like it if you kept a close eye on him. He's got a nice bump on his head and I tried to discourage him from driving, but he's a little stubborn. Can you do that, or do you want me to come and get him?"

She nearly said hell yes, come and get him, but she found herself saying she'd keep an eye on him. When she hung up, she stared at the man sleeping in her bed.

"This is just stupid. What the hell were you thinking, Kerry, to let a man you hardly know come in here and then agree to watch him sleep? In your own bed?"

She was exhausted and wondered if he would be there all night or would get up and leave soon. When ten o'clock came and went, she knew she was going to be stuck sleeping on the couch. As much as it was comfortable sitting on, the stupid thing wasn't all that comfortable to sleep on, as she discovered an hour later. She sat up on the thing and glared at Reed as he slept on.

Grabbing her pillow, she shoved it between them and lay down. Almost as soon as her head hit the pillow, she was feeling relaxed enough to close her eyes. But no matter how hard she tried to fight off sleeping to make sure he didn't move over and do whatever she was thinking she shouldn't let him do, she felt her eyes get heavier and heavier. She reached for her alarm clock, thinking she'd only lay there for an hour, and lay back down. She was nearly asleep when she thought she heard him chuckle. But she was too tired right now to care. Sleep claimed her.

CHAPTER 6

"Death, where do you suppose she's gone?" He looked over at Dora and tried not to cringe from her again. The last time he'd done that she'd sulked for a week. He didn't need that right now.

"How the hell should I know? I've not seen her since she came here the other day and talked to you guys." And the day he had told her what he wanted in exchange for not putting the pictures on the web. If he didn't count attacking her in the lot, that was. What the fuck had happened there he was still trying to work out. "I'm not her fucking keeper."

She smiled at him. No matter how mean and cruel he was to her, she loved it. He realized at that moment that she liked it rough in bed too. He'd slapped her a few nights ago and she'd cried out. It had taken him nearly five full minutes before he realized that she'd come and not been in pain. Fucking cunt. He wished he'd never met her and only the father. But he was bad enough.

"She'll need to turn up pretty soon. I need her to spot me some money for the electric and gas. She's behind from last month too."

Death looked at her. *These people are worse than me*, he thought. At least after he got what he wanted from Kerry he was going to give her what she wanted in return, the thumb drive. These two only took and took until she was nearly dry. Then they wanted more. He stood up when Dora started rubbing his cock. As much as he hated to admit it, he didn't want to fuck her any more.

"I'm going out." He picked up his coat and moved to the door before she could comment. Norman came out of the kitchen just then and he looked at him. It wasn't even ten in the morning and he had a bottle of beer in his hands. The man tipped it at him.

"Are you going to look for Kerry? If so, tell her we're running low on food." He winked at him. "We actually got our card filled back up yesterday, but no sense in telling her that. Those things don't buy us the finer things in life, like beer and smokes."

Death walked outside and into the cold morning. He wanted to run but needed to get out of this area first. His wolf snarled at him to do it now, but he calmed him with the thoughts of what he was going to do for him when he had all the money he could ever need. He smiled when he thought of the look on Kerry's face when he showed her the drive. He made his way to his home, a cave high in the mountains above the town.

"I've been watching you," he'd told her. She looked up at him while she'd been standing next to her car that night. "You can't hide from me, Kerry dear. I've got a nose for you."

"What do you want? I just want to go home. If you're here for money, you're shit out of luck. I've nothing to sell and the money is gone until I get paid again."

"I need for you to download all the information you have on credit cards that people make their cable bill payment with. All of it. I need more money, and since, as you've pointed out, you don't have anything to sell, you're still going to get it for me." She stared at him for a full minute before she answered him.

"I can't do that. No, that's not right, I won't do it. I'll lose my job, then where will you live? In the streets with my family? I just will not do it."

"Oh yeah, you will. You think I want to hang out with your family for the rest of my days?" He laughed at her and she'd taken a step back when he reached for her and put the drive in her hand. "You might want to have a look at those before you say no. I've got extra copies, so if you think destroying that one will get you out of this, think again. I only stay with them because of you. And if you don't do as I want, I'll kill them both and it will be on your hands. When you do what I want then I'm done with the lot of them."

She looked back at the house they'd both just come out of and when she turned back to him, he had shifted. The look in her eyes had made him realize that she'd be delicious when he took her. He also realized that she'd had no idea what he was. None of them did. He moved close enough to her to sniff her and get her scent, then he backed away. She stood there for a long time after he left her. He knew because he'd watched her, and when she finally got into her car and left, he'd followed her to her new digs and watched her through the night. He'd known the moment he saw her run that she'd do what he wanted.

Entering the cave, he stripped down and fisted his cock. He had masturbated so many times while he'd watched Kerry that he was sure that he'd not be able to come any other way than with his own hand. He went to the wall of the cave where he'd hung her pictures, all of them, and looked at his favorite. The one where she'd been in the shower shaving her long legs.

He held his cock while he remembered it. The way she'd bent over for him, her ass the shape of a heart. He gripped his cock harder when he could see her as if she were right in front of him, with her leg up on the little shelf and her hands running up and down while she lathered those long, strong muscles. When she stood up, her legs bent in a way that he could see her pussy just peeking out from her thighs, he grabbed the wall in front of him as his cock filled. Thinking of her leaning over again, this time she took his cock into her mouth. He cried out a strangled scream when his cum shot from him and sprayed the wall in front of him. He wanted her so badly he let his wolf take him to go and get her, and only just remembered that he had no idea where she was right now. But he was hard again and his wolf needed to kill.

Moving out of the cave, he moved into the city and roamed the alleys until he found what he wanted. As soon as she moved into the darkness, Death shifted again and she was his before she screamed.

"Don't. If you make a noise, I'll kill you before I begin." He tore her clothes off her and watched the moon dance over her flesh. It wasn't as creamy or as toned as Kerry's, but she wasn't where he could find her right now, and this thing would have to do. His wolf snarled at him, clawed at him until he had to give her to him. Leaning down to the woman, he bit her throat hard and let the wolf have him.

When he backed off her and waited, Death could feel the woman's fear. She was going to be weak enough soon that she'd no longer be fun to chase, but for now…. As soon as she took off running, the wolf watched her, snarling at her so she'd run faster. When she was nearly a mile from them, he leapt after her. The woman was dead before her body hit the ground.

As soon as the wolf had his fill, Death took him back. As he moved to the cave again, he made a slight detour to the creek that he knew ran past his home. When he dove into the icy depths, he felt it as if were a thousand tiny knives cutting into this body. He scrubbed off her blood, then he let the wolf do the same. Soon he was back in his cave with a nice fire going, and sated.

~~~

Reed woke because he was too warm. The room was dark, so he moved his hands down his body to take the comforter off, but nearly shot out of bed when he realized there was a body laying over him. Then he realized who it was. He smoothed his hands down her back to her ass, and nearly moaned when she shifted her body over his, and he did moan when her leg moved over his cock. Christ, this was a perfect way to get himself killed.

Trying to move out from under her seemed to be a lost cause. She was cold and he wasn't. That's when he realized that the room really was cold. He wondered if the heat had been turned off entirely or if she had the thermostat turned down that far. He didn't think it was the latter, and tried again to move out of the bed. When his hand brushed over her breast, he stilled.

She was naked.

The blanket that had been covering her had moved off her. He raised his head slightly and could see down the long column of her spine before it stopped. He wanted to tear the blanket away to see all of her, but wasn't sure how she was going to react now, and he was pretty sure she'd not let him explain that he'd only looked and not touched.

Laying his head back down, he tried to think. It wasn't until she moaned that he realized he was caressing her back and nearly to her ass. He couldn't do this anymore. He was going to take her, which he wanted to do more than he wanted his next breath, or she was going to have to move so he could get up and go out into the cold. Or take a cold shower. Either way, he needed some relief.

"Kerry? Kerry love, I need for you to move over." She snuggled closer and he swallowed hard when her leg moved up and down over his cock. "Christ, love, if you don't move off me I'm going to roll you to your back and bury myself deep into you." He knew the exact moment when she realized where they were.

She lifted her head and stared down at him. She didn't scream as he'd thought she would, nor did she move. The sheet that had fallen from her back was now pooled around his chest, and he knew that if he looked now, he'd see her breasts.

"You fell asleep." He nodded, trying to tell himself not to look down no matter how much he wanted to. "I called your brother and he said to watch over you."

"Walker?" She nodded, and he felt the sheet move across his chest. "Kerry, I'm aching. I need for you to either move off me or kiss me. Either way, I need you to make the decision now."

She stared at him for a long time, hours it seemed, before she moved. His breath caught when she pulled back, and he called himself all kinds of a fool for letting her go. He lay back on the bed and closed his eyes. When her body pressed against his, he looked at her again.

This time he did look and moaned when her nipples grazed over his flesh. "I don't know what draws me to you when all I want to do is push you away. Maybe if we have sex, I'll be able to forget you and I can move on with my life."

He didn't care what her reasons were. He ran his hands down her ribs to her waist and then cupped her ass and rolled her over him. His cock really did ache, and he pressed her over onto her back and looked down at her as he settled between her thighs.

He took her mouth, marveling again at her taste. She tasted of warm sunshine and the earth. Reed wanted more of her, and leaned down and laved her hard nipple until she curled her fingers into his hair and held him to her. He leaned up on one leg and his hand and pulled his shirt up and out of his pants, then over his chest. Kerry helped him pull it over his head.

Sitting up between her legs, he slowly moved the sheet off her. He wanted to see her, all of her, before he feasted on her. As her breasts flushed, he saw her ribs, then her navel. When the sheet caught on her hips, she lifted them up and he pulled it off her. Reed knew for as long as he lived this was going to be his best memory of her.

"You're gorgeous." She flushed, and he pulled the sheet completely off her legs and tossed it to the floor. "Christ, you're more beautiful than anything I've ever seen."

He moved to the edge of her bed and off. He stood before her, pulled open his pants, and freed his cock. Taking off his pants and boxers at the same time, he stood up and fisted his cock. He was aching to be deep inside of her, and knew that if he entered her now, it would be over almost as soon as it began. Going to his knees, Reed pulled her to the edge of the bed and laid her legs open on either side of him. He was going to taste her and wanted her to watch him. When she leaned up on her elbows, he kissed her bent knees and then looked up at her.

"I'm going to eat you." Her moan was nearly his undoing. "Then I'm going to make love to you. I'm going to come deep inside of you and mark you again. Do you know what I'm saying?"

"You want to bite me." He nodded. "I don't understand why, but I like the way it feels when you sink your teeth into me. Just thinking about it makes me wet."

He could smell her arousal and leaned in to bury his nose into her heat. She threw back her head and he lifted his head. He wanted her to watch him. He wanted to see her face when she enjoyed this. "Watch me, Kerry. Watch how much I enjoy drinking from you."

Pulling her closer to the edge of the bed, he spread her legs wider. He could see her clit, swollen with need, and he wanted more than anything to bite her there. Leaning slowly into her, he licked her from gate to clit, then worried the hard nubbin with his teeth and tongue. She rolled her hips up to him, and he suckled her hard.

Her climax screamed from her, and he lapped to catch all of her juices. She cried out again and again as he fucked her with his tongue. And when he pressed his finger into her, she rode him hard. He wrapped his free hand around his cock after gathering cream that dripped from her sheath.

He thought if he came like this he could take her easily. But when she cried out again, this time begging him to take her, Reed knew that he'd not be gentle with her this time even if he came a dozen times before entering her. Standing up, he nearly went back to her when she spread her legs wider for him and touched her clit.

"Move to the middle of your bed so we have room. I need you. Christ, do I ever need you." When she didn't move fast enough for him, he picked her up and moved her himself. As soon as he moved between her legs, she wrapped her legs around him and he slammed home.

"Reed," she screamed out his name. He moved out of her to the tip, then back into her hard. He had to tell himself that she wasn't a panther and that he needed to be careful with her, but every time he tried, she'd do something to make him forget again. When her nails sliced down his back, she arched up beneath him and he felt her mouth slide over his arm.

He wanted her to bite him. Now. He needed her to mark him in the way of their kind, and nearly begged her to when her teeth nipped at his shoulder as he pounded into her. When she cried out this time, he felt his own climax racing over his body, and before he could tell her to bite, command her to mark him, he felt her teeth sink into his flesh, and his climax roared from him as he let his panther go enough to mark her as his. He then filled her with his essence.

She screamed again. This time he knew that he'd hurt her, but he couldn't stop. He needed her to be his. When he lifted his head after a few more long hard strokes inside of her, he noticed that she had blood on her mouth. His blood. And that she was unconscious.

Instead of dropping over her in exhaustion, he leaned down over her and gathered her into his arms. He'd hurt her, he knew, and he hoped that she'd only fallen into this state from her climax instead of from the pain he'd caused her. When her eyes fluttered open, he watched her for any signs of pain or anger, but all she did was look at him with the most sated look on her face.

"I don't think it worked." He frowned at her. "Doing this to get you out of my system. I think I only made it worse."

"Worse how?" He moved her hair from her face and kissed her gently on the mouth. "How is this worse?"

"I don't think I'll be able to walk away from you as easily as I had hoped." She yawned as his heart skipped several beats. "You're not going to be so easy to forget."

As she closed her eyes, Reed knew without a doubt that she would try to leave him. Not because of anything that had happened here, but because she would feel she had to. And that he just didn't understand. He watched her sleep a long while before he got up and dressed. He had to do something to convince her that she had to stay with him. That he needed her to be with him for all time. He reached for the only person in the world he thought he could trust to help him. His mom.

I have a mate, but she's going to leave me. He sat down on the only other flat surface in the entire apartment. *I can't let her go.*

I figured her for a runner. I'm surprised she hasn't tried her best to be away from them all before now. Poor little thing. Reed frowned. His mom had known?

Why? How did you know? He looked around the tiny apartment and realized that this was where the pictures had been taken. He was going to fucking kill that wolf.

Have you read about her family? Her father and sister? He told her he had but that he would protect her from them. *They aren't going to leave her alone. Not ever. They're taking from her all the time. What do you think they'll do once they find out who you are and what you are to her?*

I don't care. They can have it all so long as I have her. He could feel his mom's fear, and then he realized what else they could take from them. *They'll tell what I am. They'll sell me out and her too if she's converted.*

I would imagine they would sell out each other if they thought there was a profit. He'd never met them but knew that his mom was right. *Does she know yet? What you are? Have you told her yet?*

No. I came here last night to talk to her, but…when I got here all I could think about was my head pounding. I never meant to fall asleep. He remembered her telling him that she'd called Walker. *She called Walker for me to see what to do. She was asleep near me when I woke too hot for the room.*

He watched Kerry while he thought about the pictures he'd seen of her. Whoever had taken them had to have been inside the apartment. He looked around and realized that it was much too small for anyone to hide in, and tried to remember the angle that the photos had come from. Reed went to the bathroom and looked at the shower, and tried to think where the man had to have been standing, and realized it was over the door. He nearly went to get a chair when he heard something. He reached for his mom when he heard it again.

There's someone in this apartment with us. He looked around the apartment but no longer up at the ceiling. He was sure that there must have been some sort of false area that allowed someone to get the angle of some of those shots.

Do you want me to send the police or your brothers? Most of them are here. As is your father. But I doubt he'd be much use, the old fool. Reed smiled at his mom. She'd been calling his dad that for his entire life.

Neither for now, but…I have to get her out of here before whoever it is…. Christ. I need Ama. Can you send her to me?

Twenty minutes later Ama was at the door, and he let her in. She smiled at him, and he looked up at Sebastian. He knew that he'd come too, so wasn't really surprised to see him. He went to the bed to wake Kerry. She looked up at him, and he watched her face to see if she was pissed or not. She smiled.

He leaned down and nipped at her shoulder as he spoke to her through their connection. *The man that took the photos of you is here now. Can you...my sister-in-law is going to make it so he can't see us. Can you get dressed quickly and pack whatever you're going to want to keep?*

He's here now? He nodded, marveling slightly that she'd taken him talking to her this way so easily. *Is it Death?* He didn't know who this Death person was and nearly asked her if he was a wolf, but didn't think she'd understand just yet. He kissed her shoulder as she sat up on the bed.

I'm not sure who it is. I can't even tell if it's the same...person from the lot. Ama said she can hold him for a little while, maybe ten minutes, before he would realize that something was wrong. Can you do it? She nodded, and he turned to Ama and Sebastian. The two of them closed their eyes and he helped Kerry from the bed. She hurried to the bathroom with the sheet around her, and he went to the dresser to get whatever he could.

There were no photos. None. Not of her or her family. There was a small dish on the top of the dresser with about forty-five cents in it and nothing else. There was very little in the drawers too. He gathered everything up in them and was putting them on the blanket that had ended up on the floor when she came out of the bathroom. She had on a bra and panties, and he growled low at her.

"Why do you do that? I've noticed that your brothers do as well." They both heard Sebastian laugh in the kitchen, and she flushed. "I didn't know they were here. I thought she was coming, not that she was already here. You should have told me that right away, damn it." She started pulling on the things he'd laid out for her, still glaring at him the entire time.

"They're here." He kissed her nose. "What else do you want to take? I've emptied all the drawers and I've looked, but there doesn't seem to be any photo albums or even pictures. Did I miss them?"

"No you didn't. I couldn't afford anything like that even if I did want to keep pictures of them. There's nothing. I don't have much because I can't afford it." She glared at him, and he knew that whatever he said was going to be a trap, so he simply picked up the blanket and tossed it over his shoulder. Taking her hand, he led her to the door and out into the hall. He was at his truck when he realized that she was headed to her car.

"He'll know that it's yours, and I wouldn't doubt that he has a tracker on it. It's what I would do." She looked at the car, then at his truck. "Come on. Let's get going."

"I need for you to take me to a hotel. I'll be fine there." He didn't answer as he helped her into the cab of his truck. "It can't be an expensive one, but it can be nice, just not too nice."

He nodded, knowing that it didn't matter the cost because she was going to his house. Smiling as he rounded the truck, he wondered what she was going to do when he told her what he was.

CHAPTER 7

Dora tried to call her sister again. Damn it all to hell, where was she? She picked up the useless cell phone again and tried to decide whether she'd feel better if she threw it at the wall. The stupid house phone wasn't her nice cell phone, and she hated that she had to stand in one room to use it. But Kerry had told her that she'd not buy her another cell phone if she broke another one, so she was stuck with this one.

"What happened to the money for the phone bill anyway?" Dora looked at her dad when he spoke. "I thought she gave you money for it a few months back. Did you pay it or not?"

"No. She should know better than to give me money for something as important as this. This is her fault, and now I can't get in touch with her to fix it." She tossed the phone on the table without harming it. "This is so like her to try and teach me a lesson. I need for her to pay the bill so I can talk to Death."

Her dad walked away. He was useless too. She thought of all the things that Kerry had been slacking on lately and wondered what was up her ass. First it was moving away without telling her where, and she'd had her number changed too and not given it to any of them. Then there was the job. What the hell had she been thinking when she'd given up her commission job? That money was something that Dora depended on monthly, and now it too was gone.

"Stupid girl. Why doesn't she just do what I want her to do without all these lessons? I didn't care for school when I had to go, and I don't want to learn now." Dora flopped down on the couch. "We need new furniture, and I'm betting she tells me no on that too."

Kerry had never been a very good sister. She'd always wanted to do things on her own, where Dora wanted things done for her. The first time she'd noticed that she and Kerry were so different was in grade school.

Dora had wanted a pair of tap shoes. Not that she'd take the classes for them, but because they had sounded pretty when she walked. And the boys noticed her too. As did the girls. They would be so jealous of her that she begged Kerry to lend her the money. "Lend" to her meant that she'd get what she wanted, and if you were stupid enough to give in to her, that was your loss. But Kerry had figured it out and hadn't budged on giving the money to her. Dora had stolen the shoes and had gotten caught. Kerry, the only one with any money, had paid her fine and had gotten her out. Her dad had blamed Kerry for the incident and made her promise that she'd never turn her sister down again.

"It could be really bad for you if I tossed you out on the street as young as you are." He'd been so drunk that Dora had been able to make him say that to her, and Kerry had been paying ever since. Until lately.

Now she was slacking off as if the promise, held over her head for all these years, no longer meant anything to her. Dora looked up when someone knocked on the door. She waited for her dad to come and answer it, and finally, when the person knocked again and again, she got up off the couch and went the few feet to the door to open it.

There was a beautiful man standing there. He took a step back when she reached out to touch him.

"I'm here on behalf of Kerry Stephens. Would you be Dora Stephens?" She nodded at him, thinking her sister had finally come through. "Is Norman Stephens here as well?"

"Sure, I guess he is. Do you have my money?" The man smiled at her, and Dora had a moment of panic. There was something very frightening about him. She took a step back when he asked if he could come in. She shook her head.

"Oh come now. I need for you to invite me in. You really want to." She took another step back when she touched the couch. "Come on, Dora. I'll give you all the money I have from your sister."

Dora looked at the man's hands as money suddenly appeared there. She wanted it, but...she looked at him again and saw something...shift, she supposed, around him. She shook her head.

"I don't want it." She started for the door to slam it into his face when she heard her dad coming. "I want you to go away now."

Her dad was drunk, and she could smell it on him. When the man tried to get him to invite him in, her dad shuffled by him without a word and flopped down on the couch. He was snoring in a matter of seconds.

"I'll be back, Dora Stephens, and when I do, you'll let me in or I'll simply wait for you to leave. Once I have you, you'll beg me to come inside. And I plan on coming inside of you plenty before I kill you. Death said that as his partner you and I would have a grand time together. My name is Dean, by the way. You'll want to practice saying that so when you come you'll know it." She watched the air around him become smoky, and she cried out when she felt his touch across her skin. "You'll be begging for me to take you before this is finished. Mark my words."

Then he was gone. Not walked away like she kept trying to tell her mind had happened, but simply gone. She sat down on the couch and watched the door for a long time. When she finally got up and shut it, she knew that whatever that had been was going to do just what he said. She had to figure out a way to make sure she got what she wanted before he came back. A deal for a deal sort of, one that would benefit her more than him.

~~~

Kerry tried pacing the huge room, but she ended up sitting down only after three trips. There was only the one chair in this room and less furniture in the other rooms. The only room that she'd come across that had anything in it, besides the kitchen, was the bedroom. And she'd been avoiding it like it was her job.

And that was another thing. She had to find herself one. She had things to make payments on. Like her car. It was old and needed some work done on it, but it was hers. And now it wasn't even where she could get to it. She glared at the doorway again. She wanted Reed to come back so she could yell at him and make him take her home. When someone walked through the doorway, she nearly cried out when she realized it wasn't Reed but his brother, Khan. She wasn't happy with him either.

"If I ask you to come into the kitchen with me and meet the new cook, will you behave?" She glared at him. "He will make you a nice lunch if you don't yell at him like you did me earlier."

"I don't know him. You I don't like, so he might be safe." She walked behind him. "Where is Reed? I need him to get here and take me to my home. I have things I have to do today."

"He's at the police station. They had to have someone come in and file a report of the break-in at your apartment." She shivered when Marc had shown her pictures of the ceiling above her apartment. Someone had been living up there for weeks, he'd told her. And he'd made himself at home too.

"They don't know who it is, do they?" Instead of answering her, she was introduced to Mr. Camps. He said he was pleased to meet her.

"Mistress, what would you and the master of the house want for dinner tonight?" Kerry looked at Khan, then at the cook. "I can have whatever you want ready when you're ready."

"I don't have a clue what Reed will want to eat. But I plan to be gone before then." She looked at Khan when he cleared his throat. "You have some information that you'd like to share with me and the nice cook here? If so, spill it."

"Your apartment is now a crime scene. You won't be able to go there again until they are finished with it. I'm sorry. I should have told you sooner. But I thought you knew." She nodded, not wanting to have a fit in front of Reed's cook. When they both looked at her, she felt anger surge in her, and she turned on her heel and walked to the living room again. She was brushing away the tears that kept falling when Reed touched her mind.

What's the matter? Are you all right? She'd wanted to scream at him that she certainly wasn't all right, but didn't. What would be the point?

I want to know how you can talk to me this way. I've gone my entire life without being able to speak to anyone this way, and all of the sudden you come along and now I can. What's different? She didn't expect him to answer her, or at the very least tell her the truth. She was used to that from people.

I was going to explain it to you tonight after dinner. But.... She sat down, not sure she really wanted to know. *I'm your mate, and you're mine. Do you know what that means?*

No. You've said that to me before. I take it has something to do with sex and that you bit me.

It does. A great deal more than that, but for now it will be enough. We're a mated couple. And because we bit each other and drew blood, it's opened up a path, a link I guess you could call it, that makes it so we can speak. She tried to digest this when he continued. *I can also feel your every emotion. As you can mine.*

Why? Not why did we have sex...actually, why did we have sex? I mean, why did it seem like I was going to die if we didn't, and why do we have it all the fucking time?

She wanted to ask him if he enjoyed it as much as she did, but was pretty sure he did. The way he roared out her name, the way he.... She decided that thinking about sex right now wasn't a good idea.

I can feel your arousal, Kerry. Just like it's my own. I know when you're afraid, when you're sad and hurt. I can even tell when you're pissed. I can't, however, always tell what it's about.

She didn't want anyone to know her every emotion. What would be the point? *This is not explaining anything to me. This is making me more confused and pissed off. It's bad enough that I can't go home until the police are finished with my apartment, but I'm living this...this wild, overwhelming life with a man I don't know a thing about.* She looked around his living room. *You have more space in this one room than I do in my entire apartment. What am I supposed to do all day? I can't work. I don't know anyone to call. What the fuck am I doing here?*

I'm a panther. A werepanther, as a matter of fact. And since I've claimed you, you're my mate, my other half. She didn't like the sound of that, but before she could say anything, he continued. *I'm sorry, love, but we were fated to be together, and now it's my job to protect you and keep you safe.*

And what do I do all day long while you're out storming castles and slaying dragons for me? Be at your beck and call? Be naked when you come home and let you simply fuck me? She stood up to pace. *That's simply not going to work for me. I had a life before you came along, and I'm pretty sure I can manage one after you're gone.* She felt his anger. *And you can take your being pissed off at me and shove it up your ass. I'm not your...your whatever.*

You'll do as I command you, or so help me, Kerry Bowen, I'll beat your ass and tie you to the bed.

She felt her anger boil over and her body tingle with it. She knew that he felt it too, and heard him saying her name.

Her vision blurred for several seconds. Then she felt her body tighten and ache. Throwing back her head in pain, she screamed. Every muscle in her body felt as if it were tearing apart. Then she felt hands on her body. Someone was screaming her name again, but she couldn't focus on whom. When she felt sick to her stomach, she leaned over and spilled up her belly, and then everything went black.

~~~

Kerry opened her eyes slowly. She hurt, and in so many places right now that she was sure that she'd been run over by several cars and even a few large trucks. When she tried to lift her hands up, she felt weighed down, and looked down her body. She saw then that she was in a hospital.

"You're tied to the rails. Let me untie you." She looked up at the elder Mr. Bowen. "I think you're safe from hurting yourself now, aren't you, sweetheart?"

"Where...?" Her throat hurt. When a straw was put in her mouth, she drew hard on it and felt it soothe her raw throat. She looked up at him.

"You're in the clinic. Reed is just down the hall getting us something to drink. He'll be right back. How do you feel?" He squeezed her hand as he undid the other tie. "You gave us quite the scare there for a few days. I'm just glad that Khan was there to help you through it."

She heard the door open, and Mr. Bowen stepped back as Reed approached the bed. Kerry could see the worry on his face, and when she reached up to touch his cheek, he grabbed her hand and held it to his face. She could see tears in his eyes.

"You scared me." She nodded, not sure what had happened. "When I lost the connection with you, I thought...I have no idea what I thought. Then I heard from Khan. He said you were shifting and you were in a great deal of pain. I came to you immediately, and then when you didn't wake up, we brought you here."

"Shifting?" He nodded. "I don't...I don't know what you mean. I was angry with you for something. And then...then I hurt."

"Yes. You shifted. Into a panther. I'm not sure how that happened, if you were carrying a latent gene or if I changed you. I really don't know, but thankfully you're all right." He touched his mouth to hers gently. "Are you hungry?"

Others came into the room. She saw Khan and Walker talking and could hear what they were saying, even though she was pretty sure they were whispering. When Mrs. Bowen touched her arm, she turned to look at her and wondered if she'd help her. She was feeling extremely overwhelmed right now.

"Take deep breaths, my dear. Let it out slowly." She did as she instructed and felt calmer. Then something moved along her skin, and she looked down. There was no one there.

"It's your cat." She looked at Caitlynne. "She's coming to the surface to let you know that if you need her, she's right there. Khan says she's very beautiful and sleek. But he said she was nearly wild too."

Kerry sat up and then backed up. Reed was suddenly there and she waved him away. She needed to breathe and think, and there were too many people there to do either. When Khan ordered them all to give them a moment, she looked at Reed, hoping he'd leave her too.

"I'm staying." Khan chuckled, and she glared at him. "He's going to stay and tell you what happened to you. Then he's leaving as well. But I'm not. Not now, not ever."

"I don't like you right now." He sat on her bed, and she got up and stretched. "I don't know what you think happened at your house today, but I want you all to leave me alone."

"I can't now." She looked at Khan. "You're a part of my family. And it wasn't today, it was four days ago. You are mated to my brother, though. That's wonderful, but in order to help you through your first shift, I asked you to pledge to me. When you did, I was able to pull your cat for you, or...well, you would have died. She was tearing you up to get out and help you."

"Cat? What do you mean cat? I'm not...what the fuck is going on here?" Terror ran along her skin, and she felt movement again, like someone was touching her. She looked at Reed when he growled low.

"She's upset because you are. You have to learn to control her or she'll come to the surface when you're with humans." He took her shoulders into his hands. "Breathe, baby. Just breathe and you'll calm her down."

She put out her hand and watched her arm seem to sprout fur. Then her hand morphed and she had claws. She looked up at Reed again and tried to breathe, but she was getting dizzy. Suddenly she felt a chair being shoved under her, and her head was pushed between her knees.

A panther. She was a panther? Taking deep breaths again, she tried to tell herself she was dreaming, but knew as surely as she was sitting there that she wasn't. When Khan said her name softly, she looked up at him. He and Reed were sitting across from her.

"You're a panther. Walker thinks you're at least half panther, if not more. He said that he should have checked your blood when you were brought in the first time, but didn't think of it." She shook her head, and he nodded at her. "You're going to have to believe me. I would never lie to you about this. When you were angry with Reed, I felt your cat screaming at you. When I came into the living room where you were, you'd...you'd shifted part of your body but not all. You were screaming and clawing at your skin."

He reached into his pocket and handed her his phone after he'd turned it on. Reed pulled his chair to her and took the phone, and then showed her the first picture.

"He took these. In the event that you didn't make it or you killed him, he wanted someone to know it was you so that the family could help you."

Kerry looked at Khan, then back at the picture. She was there but not really. Her face and one arm were human, but the rest of her was panther. She took the phone from him and moved through the dozen or so pictures. It showed her in varying stages of changing, and then she was a snarling large black cat. Kerry noticed that her hand was trembling when she handed the phone back to Khan.

"Why?" They both looked at her like they didn't understand. "Why now? I mean, if what you say is true and I've had this thing in me for a long time, then why now? Why come out? Why didn't she just stay where she was?"

"Could be because you were so pissed." Reed laughed a short bark of laughter. "Sorry, but, Christ, you were pissed off. And since I'd bitten you, she knew that there were others with her and she felt safe to come out and play."

She knew she'd been pissed off, too, and tried to remember why. She looked at Reed and frowned. "You commanded me to do something. Don't ever do that again. I'm not a child, and if you ever speak to me like that again, I'll...I'll tear you up."

Khan laughed and stood up. "I'm thinking you're going to be just fine now. I'm going home. I'm exhausted and I want to hold my wife and my children." He moved toward the door before turning back to her. "Kerry, for what it's worth, I'm having Marc look for your mother. I think she's the key to what's happened. Also, you'll need to speak to Dylan and Jack. They will more than likely have some information for you as well."

When he left the room, she looked at Reed. He was staring at her, and she went to the window. She had so much racing through her mind right now she wasn't sure where to start.

"When I was little, I fell from the tree." She had no idea why that suddenly popped into her head, but she thought it was important. "I was about fifteen feet up when one of the branches I was on suddenly broke. Nothing happened to me. I should have broken all sorts of bones, but there was…did the cat do that?"

He stood up and walked up behind her. When he wrapped his arms around her waist and pulled her to him, she felt…calmed. She wanted to turn around and snuggle her nose into his throat but resisted. Barely. But when he moved her hair from her shoulder and nipped at her, she felt it all the way to her toes.

"She would have kept you from being injured too badly. Did you lose consciousness?" She nodded. "You more than likely did break a few bones and hit your head. But she healed you. I would also bet that you were never sick as a child or caught any of the childhood diseases, and as an adult you more than likely never got sick either."

She hadn't been sick. And when her family did, she had to nurse them through it as well. Kerry turned in his arms and looked up at him. She needed to know what happened now.

"Will I be able to live a normal life?" She flushed when she realized he did. "I mean, will this anger thing get out of control again? Will I simply be at the store buying milk and have the sudden urge to become something I'm not?"

"You're a cat, Kerry, now and forever. And it's doubtful that you'll shift like that again. I'll learn not to piss you off too much, and that'll help." She pulled away from him, and he let her. "Kerry?"

"I don't know what to do about you." She knew that sounded bad and tried to fix it. "I mean, you're not really my kind of date. I've never been out all that much, but being with you is too much. You're rich and handsome, and I'm just…well, I'm just not."

"Handsome is not a word I'd use to describe you, no. But beautiful, breathtaking, gorgeous are just a few that I'd call you. And rich? No, you're not rich on your own, but as of the moment that we mated you're as rich as me." She shook her head at him. "Yes, you are. You and I are together, and I've fallen in love with you."

"But I don't love you."

CHAPTER 8

Reed walked around his house like a zombie. Kerry was avoiding him, and he was her as well. But this couldn't go on. He heard someone pull into his drive and went to the door, glad to see the delivery people finally here. He tried to pull in his temper because he knew that he'd been short a lot the last few days, but last night had been the point where he'd snapped at the wrong person.

He'd never forget the look on little George's face for as long as he lived when he'd told him to get the hell away from him. The little guy had wanted him to read him a story, and he'd been thinking about his mate. Khan had come at him so quickly that he'd not had any chance to defend himself. Not that he thought he would have anyway. Monica had pulled her husband off him, as well as his dad. He'd shifted and come home to find that Kerry had taken her car, which had been brought to the house only today, and gone to the bank to make arrangements to pay off her loan when she had a job. He felt her enter the hallway behind him and didn't turn.

"I have a job. As soon as I can afford the first month's rent and deposit, I'll be moving out." He felt his cat snarl at him, but Reed didn't move. "I'm sorry to have bothered you."

She was leaving him and it was all he could think about. When he turned to ask her—no, beg her—to stay, she was gone. The first piece of furniture was being brought in, and he had to deal with that.

Two hours later, the house had what he needed. He looked around at his house, no longer thinking of it as his home. The furniture had made a huge difference, but the place still felt cold and unwelcoming. He moved to the kitchen, where he knew Kerry was. She was talking to Camps.

"I don't think I should tell you. I'm thinking you'll want to make it for me and tempt me, but I'm really not all that hungry. But I thank you." She looked at Reed and started to stand, and he asked her to please stay. "I'm just going to go and look at the paper again."

When she left the room, he sat down in her chair. A sandwich and a salad were placed in front of him. He looked up at Camps and shook his head as he pushed it away. It was shoved right back at him.

"She's not eating, sir. And if you don't, what am I here for?"

He remembered thinking she looked like she'd lost some weight and looked down at the plate. "Is she eating anything?" Camps shook his head. "How long has it been since you've fixed either of us a meal?"

"You last night. You ate half of it." He looked at the door Kerry had gone through. "She has not touched anything in over a week. I worry for her. I cannot even tempt her with sweets or drink. Her cat, sir, it's starting to feel the pain of it as well."

Reed picked up the roast beef sandwich and bit into it. It had no flavor at all for him, but he knew that Camps was an excellent cook. He'd been the undercook at the mansion in DC that Caitlynne owned. He looked at Camps when he sat down across from him.

"She is very unhappy. What do you plan to do about it and the man that calls here?" Reed looked up from his lunch. "She did not tell you? I had thought that she had, but, well the man calls here nearly every day. I do not know what he is saying to her, but when she hangs up, she goes to the yard and cries. It's a sad sight to see. The poor thing sobs and sobs. Perhaps she needs to shift and become her cat for a time to feel free."

Reed had never seen her cat. He'd seen pictures of her, but not her as a cat. He finished off his sandwich and looked at Camps. He had to do something and he had to do it now. Smiling at the man, he had a sudden idea.

"I'm going to find my mate and make love to her. I want you to fix us a meal that will be keepable. Something we can heat up later if we need to." Camps nodded. "And one of those trays you fixed for Walker and Caitlynne when they were out. Can you put it near the hot tub?"

"I can do that. Yes, sir, I can do that. I was thinking you needed a decorator. Thanksgiving is in a few weeks, and I'd like to try my hand at fixing a large meal for your family. I believe your family rotates it around and it should be your turn." Reed nodded and told him to let the others know. "And the wedding, sir? Shall I have someone get that organized as well?"

Wedding. He wanted her with all his heart. He looked at Camps and told him to get it started. "I don't have a date yet, but I'm thinking that we could have something here. This place is nice enough, don't you think?"

Camps nodded. "I shall have you a list of things we'll need by the morning. I will also make you and the lovely miss a nice carbohydrate meal to keep your energy up." He stood and started pulling things from the cabinets as he spoke. "You'll need to make sure that your mother is aware of your plans when you have them set. Your father as well. He is a man who enjoys being in the loop of things, isn't he?"

Reed stood too and smiled. Okay, things might not be finalized, but they were at least moving. He went into the living room, then up to the bedroom, taking the stairs three at a time. He had his shirt off by the time he was in their room, and he was toeing off his shoes when he heard her crying in the bathroom. He went there immediately.

The door wasn't locked, so he opened it and found her in the tub. There was no water in it and she was fully clothed, but there was a trashcan next to her and it was overflowing with wet tissues. She looked up at him when he moved into the room.

"Do you mind? I know it's your house and all, but I'm in here." She started to stand and slipped. He reached for her just as she was falling out. Christ, she felt good in his arms.

"Why are you crying?" He picked her up and took her to the bed and laid her on it. "Tell me what's wrong. Did you get another phone call?"

"How did you...who told you?" She flushed. "I mean, what calls? I don't know what you're talking about."

Reed got in the bed next to her and pulled her into his arms. This was something else he missed, holding her in the big bed. When she didn't try to get away from him, he put his leg over hers and pulled her tightly to his body. She was stiff but not leaving him.

"The person who calls you, the one that upsets you so much that you go out into the yard and cry for hours. The person who is going to be dead for pissing you off." She snuggled into his throat, and he felt his body respond. "Kerry, you're going to be naked in a few seconds if you keep that up."

Her teeth grazed over his pounding pulse, and he curled his hand in her hair and held her there. When she tried to pull back, he told her no. He wanted her, and he rolled over her, pressing her into the mattress with his weight.

"I'm not sure this is a good idea." Reed smiled at her, thinking this was a wonderful idea. "You should be doing something else."

"I like this job." He put his hand at the collar of her tee-shirt and looked at her. "Is this something expensive or something you have a great attachment to?"

When she shook her head, he tore it open. Her hands moved up his arms to his biceps, and he felt her nails dig into him. When he leaned down and licked a path over the top of one breast to the other, she moaned and he nipped at the creamy flesh before lifting his head to look at her.

"I want you." She shook her head. "I do. I've never wanted anything like I do you right at this moment."

"We're not suited." He grinned at her. "I mean it. What are you going to do with me when you need to go to a family thing? You're going to be embarrassed of me when I pick up the wrong fork or do something equally stupid."

"I doubt very much anyone would care which fork you used so long as you didn't stab them with it." She rolled her eyes at him. He nipped at her nipple that was straining at the lacy fabric. She moaned and curled her hand into his hair.

"Don't make me want you." Her voice was breathless and low. "You know that I want you as well, but this won't work out. Why do you insist on doing this?"

He reached behind her and ran his hand down the back of her pants. Her ass filled his hand and he lifted her up to him. When her legs wrapped around him, he rocked hard into her, and with his free hand, moved her bra off her breast and took the warm flesh deep into his mouth. He lifted his head before he could no longer think.

"I want you because I love you. You may not think you love me, but I think you do. You're being stubborn." When she opened her mouth, he kissed her. "Quiet, it's my turn to speak. Where was I? Oh yeah. I love you. And I want to fill you with my seed and have children with you. I want to spend the rest of my life making love to you whenever the need comes over me, and run in the woods with you. But right now I need to taste you. Lick from your wet pussy until I've made you come over and over. Then I want to bury myself inside of you and make slow love to your body, bringing you to peak until you faint away with it."

She stared up at him, and he could feel her fear. He was afraid too, but not of her embarrassing him. He was afraid that she'd never trust him, never want to share what was going on with him. He was terrified that she'd never love him. He needed her.

"If I stay here, will you tell me when you get tired of me? Will you let me know when I've embarrassed you?" He nodded, afraid to speak and frighten her again. "I'm not going to be able to stay here all day without anything to do. I need a job. I was thinking of going to work for the other cable company as a lineman. I know your family owns this one, but—"

He kissed her, cutting her off. As far as he was concerned, if she wanted to work for their competitor, he was fine by that so long as she stayed with him. When she rolled her hips up to meet his thrusts, he lifted his head again and sat up between her legs.

"You have on entirely too many clothes." He reached for the tie at her pants and slowly untied them, touching her wherever and whenever he could. "I think that in order for us to seal this deal we've just come to, we need to seal it with me inside of you."

"I like that idea too." She lifted her hips and he pulled her pants down over them, then lifted her legs up to his shoulders and pulled them off. Kissing her calves as he ran his hands up and down her legs, he smiled when she moaned at him.

"I've missed you, the taste of you." He bit into her muscle and felt it quiver under his hand. "Do you have any idea how much I want to mark you again? Bite into your creamy flesh and draw your blood into my mouth?"

"Reed, you're killing me. Please do something productive before I bash your head in."

He laughed at her. "So romantic." Laying her legs on either side of him, he opened the fly of his jeans and freed his cock. When she leaned up on her elbows and looked at him, he fisted himself and watched her face.

"You're so thick. I wonder how you ever fit inside of me." He felt his balls tighten against him when she reached her fingers out and curled them around his dark head. "I've never tasted you. Would you let me? I'd like to feel your cock in my mouth when you come."

"Christ yes." She sat up and he leaned back on the bedpost. She moved her way toward him like a cat, crawling up him until her mouth was just inches from his cock. Her tongue came out and she licked him, and he nearly came up off the bed. When she wrapped her mouth around him, Reed thought that if he lasted more than the next few seconds it would be a miracle.

She played with him at first, licking and suckling at his cock before she leaned down and took him into her mouth. With her still on her hands and knees, he tried to think how to get her to turn so he could drink from her as well when she swallowed him.

"Mother fuck, yes." His eyes rolled back in his head, and he could feel his heart pounding so hard he thought he was dying. When she lifted her head, he could only beg her to finish him, but she shook her head. Christ, she was going to really kill him. Lying down now she cupped his balls gently, and as she rolled them in her hand, her tongue worried at his opening. Curling his fingers into her hair and lifting her up, he commanded her to finish him.

As soon as she took him back into her warm mouth, he knew that she was going to make him suffer. Before he could tell her again to give him his release, she pulled away from him.

"I need to come." He nodded, unable to think beyond his cock. "Please help me. I really need to come."

He told her to lie back. As soon as she was in the position he wanted her to be, he moved over her so that his cock was at her mouth and his mouth over her pussy. When he leaned down, he told her to open for him. When she was spread before him, he leaned down and suckled her clit into his mouth and bit her.

Her release was strong and her juices flowed from her. When he felt his cock in her mouth, he began fucking her, gently at first, but that soon went to the wayside when she cupped his ass and brought him deeper. When she swallowed him this time, he knew that he was going to come this way, but before he could warn her, she rolled his balls again and he came with a roar.

She cried out her own climax as well, making him want more of her, need more of her. When she let him go, he moved around and poised his cock at her entrance. She pulled his mouth to hers and he could taste himself on her. He slammed into her, and she screamed again. Then he moved his mouth to her shoulder. She licked at his throat, and his cat roared at him to take her. When she sank her teeth into him, his cat raced up and he bit her as well, tearing into her tender skin and claiming her. Reed emptied into her. His body was spent as he lay over her.

When she giggled a few minutes later, he lifted his head and looked down. "You nearly kill me and think this is funny somehow? Woman, what am I going to do with you?"

"Run with me." His cat seemed to rub along his skin in agreement. "Come out to the woods with me and let's run."

Grabbing up his pants but not bothering to put them on, he moved off the bed. Helping her to stand when she staggered slightly, he realized then that she had indeed lost a great deal of weight. He wanted to scoop her up into his arms and hold her for what he'd put her through the last several days. Pulling on his own pants now, he asked her to get dressed, saying that he was starving.

"Then after I fill my belly, I'm going to run you down and take you to the ground. But if I don't eat first, I may have to feast on you." She shivered and he pulled her body to him. "My cat wants you so badly he can hardly stand it."

Her belly growled, and she flushed. Helping her pull on one of his shirts, he took her hand and led her downstairs. When they got to the kitchen, Camps smiled at them both.

"I've made you both a nice luncheon." He asked them to sit. "I have been experimenting with all sorts of herbs and was wondering if I could get your opinion on them."

They sampled several dips and ended up putting the different sauces on sandwiches, crackers and cheese, and even a little of the cold salmon that had been left over from last night's meal. Reed had had a meal before going up to find Kerry, but found he was hungry as well. When she pushed back her plate and claimed she was stuffed, he smiled at her. Camps was picking up their plates when she yawned for the third time.

"You need a nap." She nodded, then shook her head. "Yes you do, and I'm going to lay down with you. We have the rest of our lives to run, and maybe if you're a good girl, we'll go out tonight."

He picked her up when she staggered again and carried her up to their room. It smelled of sex and them, and he pulled off the blankets one handed and put her down into the messy bed, then covered her up. She yawned again and rolled to her side. When he got in with her, she curled around him and laid her head on his chest. Reed felt like the king of the world and let sleep claim him.

CHAPTER 9

Death hung up the phone with a growl. Where the hell was she? When the man had answered the phone, he knew it was the same from all the other times, but this time instead of putting him on hold and getting Kerry, he hung up. And had done so all three times that Death had called back.

"Fuck." He paced around the large cave and tried to think what to do. He was going to have to go to her now, and that's all there was to it. But he fucking hated panthers. Fucking cats thought they were so superior to him and his kind that he wanted to find all of them and kill them.

She had better do what he wanted her to do or else. He had plans for that money and she wasn't going to back out now or he'd do just what he had said. He looked back at the pictures that had gotten damp after the last storm that had come through. Death thought about going to have larger prints made and wall papering his place with them, but he didn't want to take the chance of anyone knowing her. Before he'd just used a regular printer, but these masterpieces needed better. He reached for his phone to call her again when his phone rang. He nearly shifted, it startled him so badly. He moved to the outside of the cave to answer.

"You're bothering my family." He didn't know who this person was and nearly hung up when the man spoke again. "You leave Kerry alone, and I'll think about not killing you."

Death wondered briefly how this person had gotten his number, but then realized what the man had said. "Family? She's mine, and I plan to take her once she fulfills her end of the deal. And she'd better if she knows what's good for her."

The man laughed. "She'll do as she damn well pleases and we both know it. Kerry is just stubborn enough to piss you off one minute and have you want to hug her the next. But you'll leave her alone, or I'll make you a very dead wolf if you don't."

Even with the laughter Death felt the finger of fear run over his skin. The man had delivered his promise and made it sound as if he would take great pleasure in killing him if he didn't do as he was told. He held his phone to his ear for a while after the call was disconnected. He wasn't just afraid of the man who had called him, but terrified.

But the more he thought of it the angrier he got. What right did that man have to order him to stand down? And who was he to tell him that Kerry would do as she pleased? She would do what he said or else. Things he had in motion depended on her coming through for him.

He sat down on the chair he'd stolen a few nights ago and looked around. The first thing he was going to get was a nice house with hundreds of acres. Then he was going to put a large fence around it so he'd have it all to himself. He couldn't wait to simply run for the pleasure of it. Then he could do what he really wanted. Gaming.

He was going to bring others like him onto his property for a large fee and let them hunt. Bringing in prey would be a little tricky at first, but he'd hire others to help him. Hunting humans for sport was going to make him rich.

Death could see it now. There would be traps for them to run into so that there would be the scent of blood. Then he'd have others, wolves like him, out there to chase them to the others, just so it didn't get boring for his customers. He even thought about having a human day, a few days a month where he'd bring other hunters in, men and women who wanted to hunt their own kind using guns and knives to kill.

Smiling, Death was glad now that he'd decided to have people start calling him Death. It sounded so fear-inducing, and he liked the way it sounded when he told people. His real name, Gilbert, sounded so...ordinary, and he hated it.

"I'm going to just go by Death and people will be impressed." He laughed as his voice echoed along the walls. This was going to make him famous and extremely rich. But only if Kerry came through.

~~~

Reed waited for Khan to say something, anything about the man he'd just spoken to. When he stood up and pulled a bottle of beer from the refrigerator in the garage where they were, Reed thought that he'd been pissed. But when he spoke, Reed let go of the breath he'd been holding.

"He's afraid. Not a little either. But...." He took a long draw on the bottle before he continued. "I don't think he's going to give it up. He seems to be a man who does what he wants and fuck the consequences. Just my opinion."

"He's right." Reed looked at Marc when he came into the garage with them. "I've found some information on our boy. He's been in and out of jail a lot since he turned

105

eighteen. Most of it was petty shit, but he's gotten to the point now where he's nearing his third strike. The last time he was in jail it was for robbery, but since he wasn't carrying a gun and he didn't make it out, he was let out with a small slap."

Reed took the beer that Marc handed him without thinking, then put it on the workbench without opening it. Kerry had told him she didn't care for the smell of beer because of her dad. He wasn't going to mess up the chance to kiss her later if he could help it.

Sebastian came out while they were talking about Gilbert's nickname. He had a tray of sandwiches. "Kerry said if we were going to pretend to work on stuff out here, we should have something to eat. I get the ham on rye. She put hot peppers on it for me."

Reed figured she knew they weren't working on his bike. First of all, the thing was nearly brand new; and secondly, how many men did it take to put a license plate on one bike? He shook his head as he watched his brothers sort through the food. She'd not just sent out sandwiches, but also a couple of bowls of salad, along with a pie. Camps made the best apple pie in the world.

"Did she ever tell you what he wants her to do?" Reed looked at Dylan as he stuffed a dill pickle in his mouth whole. It was something he'd done as a kid and had gotten his ass taken to the wood shed over.

He wondered when Dylan had joined them. Looking around, he realized they were all there, and wondered how they knew. When his dad came out a few minutes later, Reed laughed. They were a family through and through.

"I think I might know." They all stopped shoveling food into their pie holes and looked at their dad. "She said she was not going to be able to get those numbers for him.

She didn't say this to me, mind you, but to the phone. I didn't realize she was on it when I picked it up in the living room."

"What numbers?" Dad shrugged at his question. "You think he wants her to get codes?"

"Or credit card numbers." Walker sat on the workbench as he continued. "Caitlynne had a case before she left. She was telling me how this man had his wife work for a large hotel chain. She'd keep the credit card numbers with all the information on them and bring them home. They were pretty clever, she said, in that they didn't spend a great deal on them, just enough to keep the bank happy and the customer in the dark."

"How did they get caught?" Reed knew the answer to Sebastian's question and told him. "You mean they stole the president's number too? Who the hell would do that? Morons?"

"Apparently. The president wanted to buy something for Marshall and he wanted to keep it personal. When he had to pay for the gift, there was another charge for nearly the same amount from the same store. When he disputed the charge, the credit card company went to the store to ask for video. I don't remember all the details, but it showed them buying things and the clerk letting them pay without the benefit of a card. She lost her job as well. And it later turned out she was their daughter-in-law and had done this several times."

"So we think he wants her to steal numbers and give them to him." Khan shook his head. "How would that even be possible now? Firstly, she doesn't work inside; and secondly, she won't do it."

"No, not unless he has photos of her in the nude he's holding over her." Reed got up to pace. "You think that's all he has on her? I mean, they're not all that good of pictures, and most of them you can't tell it's her anyway. I'm betting there's something else."

"He said he'd kill my sister." They all turned to the doorway when Kerry spoke. "I didn't think he'd really do it at first. But then about three months ago he hit her. She ended up in the hospital for nearly three weeks before she could come home. He'd broken her jaw and five ribs. There were enough cuts and bruises on her body that she'd had to have a nurse come in twice a day to change her bandages. He told her that it was my fault. That had I done just what he wanted then she wouldn't be hurting. That time he only wanted money. I had to sell my…I had to sell some things before I could pay him."

"What did you sell?" She looked away and Reed moved toward her and pulled her face around to look at him. "Tell me, love. What did you have to sell that meant so much to you?"

"My egg collection." She looked around the room and flushed. "I collected Faberge eggs. Not the really expensive ones, just what I could afford. When I sold them, I told him that I was finished with him. And if he wanted to kill my sister, I'd make sure he went to trial for it. But he only laughed at me."

"How much did he take?" She looked at his dad and shook her head. "I gotta know, love. Because when I find the bastard, I'm going to make sure that every dollar he stole from you is paid back in pain. And if'n you don't tell me, I'm gonna make up a number and extract that much from him anyway. It'd be my pleasure."

Kerry laughed, and Reed held her in his arms. Dad asked her again, and she finally told him. Dad staggered back a little before he nodded.

"Never knew that they were worth all that. You should see the collection of them that my Corrine has. Nice one too, but then she's been collecting for a great deal longer than you had. You still collect them?" She shook her head. "Shame that. So he kept on stealing from you even after you paid him off. It's going to be my utmost pleasure to make the bastard pay. Yes, sir, he's going to know that George Bowen means business."

When they all went into the house, Camps had dinner about ready. He told him that the misses, all of them, were on their way over and were bringing things.

"I do not know exactly what they are bringing, but I was assured there was no food involved. Miss Caitlynne said that she would leave that up to me." The man laughed nervously. "I'm glad, sir. She does not know her way around a kitchen, if you know what I mean."

He did. Reed had stayed with them a few times when in DC and had seen her burn popcorn. Not just once but every time she cooked it. And it mattered little if she had microwaveable kind or the stove top variety; she burned the shit out of it.

Dinner was noisy and loud, just like they all loved it. When Camps reminded him about the dinner they'd been planning, Reed asked his mom if he and Kerry could host Thanksgiving this year.

"Oh my yes. What a great idea." She looked at Kerry talking to Sebastian. "Does she cook?"

Reed laughed. "No, Camps said he'd do the cooking with her help. I'm thinking she can peel potatoes and stuff like that. Kerry doesn't know yet."

He reached into his pocket and pulled out the ring and handed it to his mom. His dad had helped him pick it out a few days ago. Not that he needed his help, but Reed was going into town to get one for her, and his dad had hitched a ride. The man had been driving him insane since.

"She'll love it." He hoped so. "When do you plan to ask her? Soon I hope. She'll need the extra that a lovely ring can give her when she goes up against her family. They are somewhat of a pain in the ass, aren't they?"

"You don't know the half of it. The sister and her father came to my office when I was getting it set up on one of the buildings on Maple. Dora said she'd heard I was dating Kerry. Told me to tell her that the bills were piling up and asked her to pay up."

"What on earth? Did you ask her why she wasn't paying her own bills? And what was her father saying when this was going on? Don't tell me the man encourages this sort of thing."

Not only had he encouraged it, but was mad when Reed wouldn't give them cab money to pay the driver. He remembered the conversation he'd had with the two of them and still couldn't believe what they'd said and done.

"How do you propose that we pay him then? I've no money now that Kerry has decided to cut us off. And then there is her sloppy payment history. She'll ruin our good name if she doesn't pay them on time. I've told her time and time again that having a good credit history is the only way to go."

"You have a good credit history because she pays your bills on time?" Norman had actually looked proud of that. "Un-fucking believable. Why don't you have a job and pay your own fucking bills? You look fit enough, if you discount the fact that you're a drunk and a bastard."

"Now, you see here. You can't talk to me that way. We're just here to get what is due us from Kerry. She is our provider and always has been." Norman looked around his office, and Reed could see the greed come into his eyes. "Maybe if you give me some money I can leave her be for the time being, until she gets back up on her feet anyway."

"No."

Norman laughed. Then when Norman realized that Reed was serious, he frowned. The look on his face was priceless, and Reed wished that he'd had his phone out.

"You mean she's not off her feet and is working again? That's good to hear. We should be hearing from her…. Why are you shaking your head, young man? Either she's up and about or she's not."

Reed grinned. "She is up and about. She isn't working, however, at the moment. And even if she was, you're not going to get anything else from her. She's done with the both of you."

"She's not allowed. Tell him, Dad. Tell him that she has to help us. It's what she was brought to us for." Dora's mouth snapped closed, and still a day later, Reed couldn't figure out what she'd been saying. His mom touching his arm brought him from his musings.

"She's upset." He stood up and went to Kerry. She was just coming from the kitchen and he took her back in there to see what had happened. She crumbled into tears when he pulled her to him.

"My father…he called here to…how did they find me?" He held her, trying to keep his own temper under control. "He said I was to send him the money right now or he'd come here and take it from me. I don't have any more to give them. And even if I did, why should I have to?"

Khan came into the kitchen with his son, little KJ. He was covered in food, and he started to leave when Kerry's next words made both of them look at her.

"Why do they keep throwing it in my face that I'm not really their kin, and I'm a Stephens because they let me be a part of them? I wish now I'd been found by someone else."

"He's not your father?" She shook her head at Khan. "Then who is he and what is his relationship to you? I mean, do you know anything about your biological parents, anything at all?"

"No. I mean, my birth certificate didn't even exist until I was five. They had to have one for me to go to school, and when Dad took in all the paperwork to have one made, they had to leave a few things blank. It's the reason I have a hard time proving anything. None of the information on it is actually true." She pulled away from Reed to go to her bag and handed him a copy of it. "See the date? That's about a week before I started in first grade. According to my dad, someone came to the door and told him that he could have me if he wanted me. Apparently, he said that I could be free labor for the rest of my life and would take care of them both."

"Do you believe him?" She told him she didn't. "Then why are you still caring for them? You've not lived at home since you were eighteen at least. Why are they still making you do things for them?"

"Because when I don't, they make my life really hard; and lately Death has been coming around a lot to put me in line."

CHAPTER 10

"That was bill collectors again. Apparently my family has given them this number. They are demanding that I pay for their services or my family will be shut off." Kerry looked at Camps. "That just breaks my heart that they don't have phone service."

He laughed and set a plate of eggs and ham in front of her. He'd told her yesterday that since the dining room furniture had arrived, she should eat in there and he'd find someone to serve her. She told him if she couldn't eat in the kitchen with him, she'd have to not eat. He smiled, the old softy.

"Master Bowen Senior will be here shortly. He said that you and he had a date." She'd forgotten about that. He was taking her to the cable office to see if she could help them out with a few bumps.

"He's a nice man. And I really like Corrine." She'd been told in no uncertain terms to call them by their first names. She had been embarrassed at first, but enjoyed them too much not to do as they had asked.

"When he would come to the mansion in DC, he would tease my missus." Camps smiled. "Sometimes he would make her laugh even when she didn't feel well."

"I'm sorry that she passed away. I've heard great things about her." He nodded. "Reed tells me that we're having Thanksgiving here. You need my help?"

She nearly laughed at the expression on his face, but he turned away quickly. Burn one hamburger and the kitchen was off limits. Not that she cared. Kerry hated to cook.

"I can peel potatoes or chop up lettuce if you want. And grate things without losing my fingers now, thanks to you." He turned back and smiled at her. "I would never try to cook anything again. I promise."

He nodded. "I have a menu planned out. If you would have time to look it over, I can start on some of the things we can freeze beforehand. Then there is the turkey. I'll have to place an order for one now for the size we'll need for you all."

"My family never had Thanksgiving dinners. I would have had to make sure they had all the ingredients and then cook it. I'm not sure who cooks for them now, but when I lived there, we had a lot of meals that were already precooked. With working and taking care of them and school, I didn't have a lot of time to figure out cooking too." She looked over the neatly written menu. "I was wondering if you could add something. I really like those pull apart rolls you make for us. I guess baked bread is what the family wants though. Never mind."

He took the menu from her and marked out bread and wrote pull apart. "It is in this household and you are mistress here. We will have what you wish."

She laughed and looked up when George knocked once and came into the kitchen. Reed was working with the police this morning on a murder or he would have taken her. The rest were going to meet them at the office.

"Ah, there is my favorite newest daughter-in-law. I was wondering if you'd pretend to be a little late getting ready so I can persuade Camps here to make me one of those amazing omelets that he makes." He winked at her then looked at Camps. "You have the stuff I love, don't you, old man?"

Camps set a plate with an egg white omelet and dry wheat toast on it in front of George. "The missus called me last night and said to give you this. She said if I gave you anything else that she would strip me naked and pour honey over me and put me with the red ants she found in the yard last week. She is very frightening."

George looked at the food, then at Kerry and back to the food. "A man could die wanting for a good meal when he reaches a certain age. I've lived this long eating what I damned well want." He pushed the food away. "Damned women. It's getting so a man can't have a good time anymore without someone telling him that it's bad for him."

She grabbed her coat and was following him out the door when Camps stopped her and handed her a covered dish. With a wink, she was out the door and in the warm limo. She handed him the dish and he smiled.

"Knew you were my favorite when I met you." He ate the bacon first and then picked up the omelet and ate it in three large bites. "You've no idea how they're starving me in my own home. Why, just the other day I was told that for my afternoon snack, I had to eat vegetables. Vegetables, I tell you. I'm a damned panther. We don't do vegetables."

She was still laughing when the limo took a hard turn. Holding onto the strap, she watched as George pressed several buttons. She assumed he was trying to get the window down. When he looked at her, she saw fear and it spiked up her own. For him to be afraid, there was double reason for her to be.

What is it? Reed sounded so frantic that she almost told him nothing. *Dad is with you and he's talking to Khan. Where are you?*

I don't know. In the limo. We were going to the cable office. The car took another sharp turn, and she felt a little sick from it. *I don't think we're going to make it if he keeps driving like this.*

Stop and think, honey. Can you see anything? Out the window? The driver? She told him no, the windows were dark and wouldn't work. *How long have you been in the car?*

Less than ten minutes, I guess. The car is a dark one, almost black, but it's really blue. There are four doors, and the driver isn't tall. I'd say maybe a few inches shorter than me. White, with one of those...Reed, I think it's Robbie from work. She closed her eyes when they took another turn. *We've made two lefts and a right. We're going really fast and he's taking the curves on two wheels, it feels like. My phone. Let me see if I can pinpoint us.*

Her cat snarled at her, and she was afraid she'd shift. It had hurt so much the last time that she'd not wanted to ever do that again. Getting her phone to work proved to be sickening because of the way he was driving. When she finally got it to work, she told Reed where they were.

Brilliant, love, brilliant. Dad is going to shift if anything happens where you're in trouble. He's bigger and meaner than you are right now because he's pissed off. When the door opens, move to the other door and wait. We're on our way.

When they came to a sudden stop, she watched as George was slammed against the window that separated the front from the back and broke it. She looked at Robbie when he turned around, and she saw his smile.

"Hello, Kerry. You and I are going to have some fun and then you're going to get my job back for me." She looked at George and knew that he wasn't going to be any help. When the door opened to her right, she tried to go to her left, but that door opened suddenly and she was being pulled from that side. When she landed in the dirt, she looked up at Russ. He had a gun and he didn't look all that happy to see her.

"What do you think I'm going to be able to do for you if you fucking kidnap me? I'm not going to be able to get you a job at a fast food restaurant after this." She lunged for the gun only to have it hit her in the head. Her cat snarled at her, and she tried to hold her back. But when she was jerked up and held by Robbie, she let her take her.

~~~

George held the young cat. She was terrified, and he didn't really blame her. He'd seen what they'd done to her and what she'd done to them, and he'd been unable to do a damned thing about it. When she raised her head to look at him again, he felt his heart break for her.

"It'll be all right, dear. I swear to you it will. You'll see as soon as Reed and the others get here, they'll fix this right up." He hoped so anyway. He looked at what was left of the two men and certainly hoped so.

She'd killed them both, sure enough. And she'd done it quickly and with a viciousness that had him both impressed and terrified. When he'd stumbled out of the back of the limo, he was ready to let his own cat take him when the man had hit her, but she'd shifted so quickly that all he could do was watch. Then as suddenly as it started, it was finished. She had limped to him and he'd held her as he called for his sons to come now.

The first truck that pulled up had her bouncing to her feet and standing over George. The fur on her back was standing on end, and he was glad, gladder than he'd ever been in his life, to see the men stop and wait for her to recognize them.

"She's a mite on edge. I'd move slowly if I was you. I don't think she'll attack you, but…well, she's a little on edge." Reed nodded, and Khan went to his knees. "Khan, you didn't call the police, did you?"

"No, sir." George nodded and knew his sons were trying their best not to let their own cats go with all this blood around them. "Did she do this, really?"

"Yes. And now she's frightened." Reed moved closer to her, and she snarled. "Go easy, boy. She's protecting me again."

"What happened, Dad?" He showed Reed the blood on his shirt. "They hurt you? Shot at you?"

"I don't think that was their intention, but when she…she saved them from killing me is what she did. And she's hurt too. Think they might have shot her in the leg. She can't shift on account of her not having things to pull on, but…." He took a deep breath. "She was fucking amazing."

The next truck pulled in and George's mate leapt out of the cab. She moved toward them and Kerry snarled again. When Corrine dropped to her knees in front of Kerry, she pulled the cat into her arms and held her, sobbing.

When Corrine looked at him, he would swear he fell in love with her all over. "You old fool. What am I going to do with you?"

"She said you'd be a mite upset with me." He tried to move, but he was hurting more now. "I'm thinking she'll let you go by now. I think I might need Walker. She might too, if I'm thinking right."

He was light-headed and tried to remain upright. He knew that he could shift and be all right, but he'd had to keep her from running. Because he knew she would have. When he felt hands on him, he looked up. He didn't remember lying down, but now that he was there, he didn't feel much like getting up.

"Been shot again, damn it. How many bullets does an old man gotta take before he can have real food?" He knew he was babbling, but he was a little afraid. He'd never felt like this before. "Do you think later I can have some bacon?"

"You can have whatever you want if you live. What the hell were you thinking, not shifting? What am I going to do with you?" He smiled at her, and he felt a tear hit his face. "Don't you dare die on me, you turd."

"I don't plan on it, but sometimes things like this happen." He opened his eyes when Khan shouted at him. "Do you mind? I'm very tired."

"Shift, damn it." He wanted to tell Khan it was too late, but he felt his cat move along his skin. "Shift now."

The cat took him, but he really did think it was too late. He knew that he was bleeding badly, but the girl...she would have run and he wasn't going to lose her. She had given him the best breakfast he'd ever had. He blinked several times.

"Can you get up?" He shook his head. "Come on, Dad, you have to move him around so he can heal you. Lying there is not an option."

I hurt. It wasn't as hard to admit as he'd thought it would be and was glad for it. *I can't do it. I'm old and out of shape.*

"If you make what I did for you count for nothing, I will tell little George what a coward you were. That you lay in your own blood and gave up." When Kerry spoke, George looked at her, sitting next to him with Reed's shirt on. "You old bastard, get the fuck up and help me clean this mess up. I would be basking in my mate's arms right now if you could just show a little gumption."

Gumption? You want gumption? I'll show it to you. He struggled to stand and snarled at Khan when he tried to help him. *You know what I'm going to do when we get your bottom back to the house? I'm going to tell my Corrine that you force fed me a breakfast that you knew I wasn't to have. See what she thinks of that.*

He was feeling a little better but still weak. He looked at her and wanted to continue being pissed off at her, but she was smiling and he thought it the best thing he'd see in an age. When she brushed at her cheeks, he moved toward her and rubbed his head on her throat and licked at the tears. Not even the low growl from Reed could have made him stop loving this girl.

You saved my life. Worthless as it is, I'm grateful to you. She nodded. *You did a good job here today, love. Had you not, both of us would be dead and none would be the wiser for our passing.*

George watched his sons move around the two bodies. He went out to the deeper part of the woods and shifted, and pulled on the clothes that were always in the truck. He held his Corrine as the others discussed what to do with the two dead men.

Ama looked at them, then at the men. "I can take care of the back of the limo. Prints and stuff like that if you just want to leave them here. Someone will wonder what killed them and it'll come up as a large panther, but that's about all. There's no way that they can trace it back to the family, and there was already that small blurb about a panther being sighted recently."

So it was decided. They'd leave the men there to be found or not, and the car was wiped clean of all traces of

Kerry and George. George watched Reed fiddle with the GPS to take off that they'd been to his house, and they loaded into the trucks and moved out. When the one in front of them stopped suddenly, George had another fright, but Ama got out and moved to where they'd been and waved her hands around. He watched as the grass and dirt covered their tracks.

"I think she's a good one to have on our side." Corrine nodded and put the container from the breakfast he'd had in the back of the limo in his lap. "I can explain."

"I just bet you can. What did I tell you? What did I tell that cook? You are to be on a diet. I don't want a—"

He kissed her. George had seen his sons do the same thing and had always wanted to give it a go, but hadn't had the opportunity until then. When she moaned at him, he felt his old body stir to life. The groaning from the others in the truck had him pulling away. With a wink, he took his Corrine's hand and held it. No more was mentioned about the food he'd been smuggled.

"You think Death sent them?" He looked at Walker, who was driving when he asked. "I don't think so, but what do you think? Did they say anything about them?"

"Nope. I was out until she'd been hit. When I came out of the ride we were in she was being held by the bigger one and the other was beating her to shit. He did mention something about a job, but I didn't understand him. You think she had something to do with him losing his license to drive that limo or some other bullshit?"

"He worked for the cable company until three weeks ago. Both of them did. The bigger man, Russ McCall, is the one that left her on her own when she was training as a lineman. The other man, Robbie Kline, is the one that lost his job for sharing information, personal information, about another employee, namely her." Dylan turned in his seat to look at them. "He shared that she was making good money and that her being out as a lineman was a man's work. I fired them both, as well as Agnes Wells. She was another of them that just had to go. I plan to see if Wells had anything to do with this too."

"So this Death person, he's not a part of this and is still out to hurt our girl?" Dylan nodded. "We have a plan? If so, then I'd like to be a part of it."

George expected them to tell him no, he wasn't, and at the very least his Corrine to tell him no, but Dylan nodded and his mate followed suit. The girl needed him, and damn it all to hell, he needed her too.

He loved all his daughters-in-law, but this girl, for whatever reasons, held his heart. Not because she'd saved him, but there was something about her that made him need to keep her close.

He leaned his head against the back window and tried to tell himself that he was okay, that he was going to be fine. But every time he closed his eyes, he could see her tearing into those men. Tearing into them like she'd meant business.

He supposed she had, too. It took something extra to tear a man's head off with just one swipe of a claw, and she'd done it. Not only had she done it, but she had done so with the other man shooting at her.

Yeah, George thought, he was going to keep her around.

CHAPTER 11

Death read about the two men getting killed twice before he tossed the paper away in disgust. They were idiots, and now that they'd put the Bowens on heightened alert, there was no way he was going to just simply go in, get the girl, and get out. He had to think of something else. Dora came into the room just as he was leaning back, and he realized that he should have left a few minutes earlier.

"The phone is off." He nodded, wondering what he was supposed to do about it. "And the electricity man said that we have seventy-two hours to get the unpaid balance paid or that will be off too. How can they just do that to us? And why is Kerry not doing her job?"

"Her job? I'm pretty sure she, like most people, thinks you should get up off your lazy fucking ass and find your own job. Why the fuck are you waiting around for her to do everything for you?" He pulled away from her when she stood up. "You'll figure this out today or I'm history. I don't need a bitch like you hanging on my shoulder. At least Kerry gets what I tell her and doesn't fuck around."

"You know she had to sell her stupid collection to get that money for you. If you'd pay her back, maybe we'd have—"

He backhanded her. It felt better than he'd imagined it would, and he hit her again. Pulling his wolf back was hard; he wanted to taste the blood that now poured from her mouth, and he wanted to kill her. Death actually thought about it, but Norman came in just then. Another sorry piece of shit.

"What have you done now?" He turned to snarl at the man and realized he was speaking to his daughter. "Haven't I told you time and time again not to bother this young man? He's our ticket, I think. Yes, he's going to get us out of the shit hole and onto bigger and better things."

"How so?" Norman looked at him. "How do you figure that I'd do anything for you? You're as stupid as she is if you think I'm going to start footing the bills around here. Go find yourself another sucker."

"But you're going to bring Kerry to heel, aren't you?" Death looked at him, ready to attack if he said the wrong thing. "Oh, I know you've been watching her. I even know that you're not human. But I don't care. Neither was Kerry's mom, for that matter. At least her mother was a panther and her father…I've no idea. Is that what you want her for, her being a cat and all? Won't do you any good. She won't shift. Not ever, according to her mom. Said she didn't have enough genes in her or some lame shit."

"Kerry's mom was a panther?" Norman nodded, and Death sat down. "Since when? And why the fuck didn't you tell me this?"

"Since birth, I would imagine. And tell you? Why, you didn't share what you were, so I thought I'd keep my little secrets as well." He started to help Dora up off the floor, but then left her there. "She's much too heavy for me, but I believe she'll be fine in a few moments. Now, where was I? Oh yes, Kerry. Her mother brought her here when she was just a baby. I suppose I should have been more suspicious about them both, but my wife had just died and I had Dora to care for. I had no idea what to do with the baby, so the woman took over her care with her own daughter."

"So she just told you?" He shook his head and laughed. "But you found out. How? And how did you end up with Kerry?"

"She...disappeared. And I'm not saying I killed her, but she won't be coming back here. She changed when...when she was bleeding. I was scared of her and, well...."

"You did kill her." Norman said nothing. "And me, how did you know that I wasn't human? I know damn good and well you never saw me shift."

"I have a friend at one of those labs. She was kind enough to tell me that your hair has canine in it. She said you were wolf, a werewolf. You can't imagine how many pictures flashed through my mind when she told me." He sat down on the couch and watched him. "Now, we are going to strike a deal, and with this deal I'm going to be a rich man."

"You're going to blackmail me?" Norman nodded and smiled. "And what's to happen if I decided I don't want to play your game and simply kill you?"

"You have no idea what I have on you, first of all. Then there is the added bonus that I've taken precautions. Very detailed precautions, you might say." He pointed to the chair across from him, and Death sat. "You really didn't think that I'm as stupid as I've led you to believe, did you? My daughter sadly is, but not me. I have prided myself on taking care of number one."

Death thought he could easily kill the man, but for the moment he couldn't. He had something up his sleeve and he would bet his last buck that it had to do with bilking money out of the Bowens. It had been his plan until the fuckwads had messed it up.

"I can get her here. For a price, mind you." Death leaned forward and waited. "She'll come here if I tell her to. Especially after what you've done to her sister."

They both looked over at Dora, who was still out. He'd hit her pretty good, and her face showed it. He doubted very much she'd die from the wounds, but she'd be pretty fucking sore when she woke up. Death had an urge to get up and hit her again, but Norman continued.

"She'll come here because you've lost your mind and hurt her. I've no way to get her to the hospital, and now that the phones are off, well, there is no way for me to call the hospital either." He smiled, and Death waited. "You'd have to leave me your phone somehow. Then I'd call her and she'd come. Right away, too, I would imagine."

"I'd just happen to leave my phone here. And how will that look? And who's to say you wouldn't call the police and tell them what I did?" Norman grinned again, and Death thought about how much he was going to enjoy tearing this man to shreds when the time was right. "You're not giving me a warm and fuzzy feeling, you prick. What's the plan?"

"Simple enough. I call Kerry and tell her you've nearly killed her sister and…and the hospital won't take her because of unpaid bills. That should have her bringing money. Plus, I don't have a way to take her. That way when she shows up, you can nab her and hold her until that man she's staying with pays up." He leaned back and looked entirely too smug. "You do like my plan, admit it."

Death did, but he had to have something out of this. He looked at Dora again and wondered what she'd say when she woke. More than likely anything so long as she was taken care of. Norman would turn him in, but the man was used to others doing things for him, and right now he needed money more than anything. Besides, if they caused him problems later, he could always come back and use them in his hunting plan. He smiled for the first time since sitting in this chair.

"I'll have to hit you." Norman looked frightened. "No one is going to believe Dora and I struggled and she got my phone. It'll have to be you, and you'll have to take it like a man." He stood and held out his phone and tried not to show how much he was going to enjoy this. "This is the way it will have to work. Especially if she's beat to hell and all."

"You're not to hit me too hard, and not in the face. I pride myself on my looks." Death shook his head, and Norman stood. "I guess you're right, damn it. Well, I suppose there has to be some pain for all this. But first, how much do you plan to ask for her?"

"Ten million dollars." His fist connected with Norman's nose immediately. He'd checked himself at the last moment, forgetting for just that second that this man was human and could die if he wasn't careful. Death leaned over the prone man and licked blood off his face.

"The better to find you later if you fuck with me." He moved to the door, dropping the phone on Norman's chest. Time to make tracks. But first he went to the man's bedroom and searched everywhere, coming up with nearly four hundred dollars. The fucking bastard had been holding out on them. He did the same thing to Dora's room and found a grand. Going to the living room where they both still lay, he smiled. He might have to bring them out to his new place anyway if this worked out. They were about as cold as he was.

~~~

"Her name is Letitia, no maiden name as yet. She was twenty when you were born, and she disappeared right around your birthday. Your actual birthday. The one on the certificate is incorrect. We're pretty sure that Norman Stephens killed her." Kerry looked up at Jack, and she sat down. "I've been trying to figure out your dad's name and finally had to go to my source. Don't ask."

"Is he dead as well?" Jack shrugged. "Did he kill him as well?" Kerry looked over the notes that Jack had handed her and looked up when she didn't answer.

"There is nothing about his death in the archives. It simply says 'presumed dead.' It's the only entry in the entire book like that. Either it says what killed them or it says they're alive. I don't know why it says that." Jack handed her a photo. "I did find this, however. I think that's your mom there, and the man is your dad. His name was Olen Hendricks. His name is on the back, but I can't read the other name. Could be anyone, I guess, but you look like her."

She did too. Kerry could see her dark hair and her startling eyes. Even in the black and white photo, she could tell that they were as blue as hers were. She ran her finger gently over the picture and handed it to Reed, and took the other picture.

"That one is a little clearer, but not much more help. I found them in the back of the file. There are more pictures of panthers with the last name Taylor, with Stephens in parentheses, but those two are the only ones attached to your name. The older woman with them in this one looks like the man, so she might be your grandmother. She is deceased. Natural causes."

"And this person that's calling himself Death, have you found out anything about him?"

Jack told her to keep the pictures as she answered Reed. "Yes. He's a loner. A wolf that doesn't belong to any pack, and he hasn't reported to the pack leader here. I would say he's been here for a few months, maybe as long as a year, but not much more than that. He hooked up with Dora Stephens about a week after coming here. Not sure what the interest is, but it happened."

Dylan laughed, and she looked at him. "You know something?" He shook his head and then nodded. "You do or you don't? I'm just scared enough right now to take you on."

"You're a mean little cuss, aren't you? Did Gilbert—because I refuse to call him Death any longer—has he ever made an advance toward you?"

Reed growled, and she looked at him. There was something so sexy about the way he would get all cat-like when he thought she had someone else. She nearly laughed, but Monica, who was in the other room, cautioned her.

He's a little on edge right now, and if you give him the slightest reason, he'll go out now and find this person and kill them. Then where will you be?

Not being chased? Not having someone kill me? I can list a dozen reasons or more to just let him stop this shit.

Monica laughed, then sobered.

And if he is a part of something bigger? What then? Will you continue to have Reed kill off everyone until you can feel safe? I have to tell you something, love, you're never going to be free of these people until you know what they want. Trust me, I know.

"Kerry? Did he?"

She shook her head. She had a feeling that all of the women of this streak had had to deal with much worse than she had. She looked at Reed and touched his face. "I'm sorry. You're being put through so much for me. I've never had anyone care for me as much as you and your family have."

"It's not hard. We love you." She kissed his mouth and looked at Dylan. "No. He never did. Why do you ask?"

"Because for some reason, he didn't try to date you. Instead, he went for your sister. Why do you think that is? You had what he wanted. The numbers, right? He wanted you to steal the credit card numbers of everyone and give them to him. That would have made more sense to have you helping him and not your idiot sister. There is something about you that...for lack of a better term, frightened him off. Much, I would assume, like the feelings we all get to protect you."

"You think that even though he wanted her, he found some reason that he couldn't have her?" She looked at Jack when she spoke. "I get it. Sort of like she has this shield around her that repels him and attracts us. But what?"

"I would imagine that only her parents would know the answer to that. But in the meantime, we have to figure out who, if anyone, Gilbert is working for. Because even though I think he's incredibly stupid, someone has to be telling him what to do. He's just not smart enough to do this alone." Kerry got up to pace. "Do you know anyone? Anyone at all that he might have mentioned?"

She tried to think, but nothing was coming. She'd tried her best to avoid Death...or Gilbert...any time she'd been with her family. He'd rarely talked to her except the one time when he'd wanted the money. She'd had to....

She turned to the table with all of them at it. "I sold off all my eggs. He had a buyer that I spoke to twice. He said that he would give me a fair price for them, but he wasn't going to give me their weight. Not their worth but their weight. Then a few months later, a man came to the house looking for Gilbert. He said that Gilbert owed him something, and he was there to collect his weight." All of them were poised for his name, but she couldn't think of it. The harder she tried, the more it seemed to slip away. She told them she couldn't think.

"Come on." She looked at Reed when he took her hand and led her to the kitchen. Camps was there, and he handed a bag to her and a basket to Reed. They were on the deck before she could find out what the hell he was doing.

"Do you realize that I've never seen you shift? You've done it twice now, and both times my family has been there to see you, but never me." He pulled his shirt over his head and laid it on the deck railing. "It's cold out. You should probably hurry."

"Hurry? Hurry and do what?" She watched as he tossed his wallet and keys onto the table that had an inch of snow on it. "What the hell are you doing?"

"Stripping. I'm going to shift and run you down and fuck you until you can't move. Then I'm going to take you again when we're humans." He stopped toeing off his shoes and looked at her. "You planning to shift dressed? I don't think there are any clothes in this basket. Maybe a blanket, but no clothes."

She took off the sweater she'd borrowed from his closet and put it next to his shirt on the rail. Then she took off her shoes and her pants. It really was cold, but not as bad as she would have thought. He winked at her.

"You burn hotter as a cat...any shifter as a matter of fact. You'll find you need less and less clothing as you figure out how to regulate yourself." She nodded and watched him as he pulled off his pants, leaving his boxers in place. "You ready for this?"

"No. I'm actually sort of afraid. It hurt me the first time I did it. When I shifted the second time…it was too fast. I don't remember it much. But now I have time to think and I'm afraid."

He nodded and told her to close her eyes. "Think of her, your cat. You should see her there. See her?" She nodded. "She's not going to hurt you, not ever. Don't think of her as you. That's why it hurts you. You're thinking too hard. Think of her as something separate from you, someone you want to have come to you. When she thinks you're ready, she'll leap at you. Let her come. Let her take you and she will."

She felt silly at first, looking for a panther in her mind, but then she was there. Kerry watched her pace back and forth, her large paws stirring snow on the ground, her breath turning the air around her white with each breath. When she sat and looked at her, Kerry felt her move over her body like she was touching her. Then she stood up and leapt forward, and in Kerry's place was her cat. She opened her eyes when Reed said her name.

"How do you feel?" Kerry looked down at the snow on the deck and wasn't surprised to see dark paws in place of her bare feet. She looked up at him and could see his cock, and moved forward and rubbed her head against him. His growl made her want him, but she knew that if he took her there on the deck, some of the fun would be lost. Leaping over the railing, she landed on the top of a concrete wall just wide enough for her to stand on.

She ran until she couldn't run any more. There were so many scents to smell and to chase. She found that she could track things; a rabbit that had been eating some of the wild grass that was under a bush; a deer that had been playing with her young. The desire to chase them all was a little overwhelming, but she knew that hurting one of them would be wrong and only looked for them. There was water to her left, and she darted for it only to find another scent, one that she didn't know but found that she wanted to stay away from. The urge to mark trees was there, but she shied away from peeing on them. When she saw Reed coming toward her as a large black cat, she still waited to see what he would do.

You've left your marks everywhere so it will be harder to find you. Unless you don't want me to chase you? She purred at the thought of him taking her in his form. *Do you know how delicious you smell to me right now? A lovely cat and all mine.*

Maybe you belong to me and I want to chase you. He seemed to grow in size, and she took a step back. *So the bigger one of us wins in this.*

Always. He rubbed his body along her side, then around the other side of her. She knew he was marking her with his scent, and she found that she needed that. When he nipped at her, the cat snarled and Kerry laughed. Reed's command to run had her taking off before she could think not to. The chase had begun.

CHAPTER 12

Reed couldn't help but marvel at her speed and grace. When she moved over fallen logs and large rocks, it looked like poetry in motion. She slid along the trees and plants without disturbing the wildlife that hid within them, and when she stopped to watch something, she was quiet and didn't try to chase down the animals that roamed their land. Then she turned to look at him, and his breath caught. Christ, he really was in love with her.

You're beautiful. I know a man really isn't supposed to be, but you are. He stood up and moved slowly toward her. *I'm supposed to be running, but I'd just like to look right now.*

She looked back to where she had been before, and he looked as well. A family of deer was drinking from the water not ten feet from them. A stag and two female, as well as three fawns. He realized that he'd never seen anything like this in the city, even though Walker and Caitlynne's property was large and well maintained. He rubbed against her again.

Will I get to ever take you like this? She purred and lay down. *I want you. I've thought about taking you this way for so long that it's all I can do not to pounce on you and make you* mine. *And my cat, he wants you as well. His need to mark you as his, you and your cat, makes him claw at me.*

I want you. But I have to say something first. She stood up and rubbed him in much the same manner he'd rubbed her. *I love you. I've never said that to anyone before, not even my family. I think I knew from the start that they never wanted or loved me. Not now, not now that I've seen and felt what a family feels like.*

This time when she lay down, he moved over her. He wanted her so bad, but for the moment he only wanted to protect her. When she snarled at him, Reed leaned down and nipped at her shoulder, and when she growled at him, he bit harder.

He mounted her. Coming up behind her now, he held her down with his paw and bit deeply into her shoulder when she tried to move. She fought him, which his cat liked, and when she tried to bite him back, he sank his teeth to the bone. She lay still then, and he felt his cock ready for her.

We can smell you. She tried once again to get away from him, and he growled. *Christ, I can't wait.*

He slammed into her and felt her tighten around him. She was his and he was going to show her. When her sheath rippled around him, he fucked her harder and felt his balls slap against her in time with his quick strokes. When she snarled at him, he jerked his teeth into her and knew that she was going to have a scar, both as human and cat.

His climax poured from him. Letting go of her shoulder, he threw back his head as he continued fucking her and roared. She came with him, he knew, and felt his cat fill her again and again until he was sated. Now he wanted his mate.

Shift, love. I need you. She moved from under him, and he watched her cat leave her behind. Reed snarled once again, but before he could shift back with her, he leaned in and licked her, tasted her dewy skin, and purred. Reed shifted.

"Take me, Reed, please. I need to feel you deep inside of me now." He lifted her up as he sat on his knees and pulled her body down and onto his cock. Her legs wrapped tightly around him, and he took them both to the ground. Taking her mouth, he kissed her hungrily, dancing his tongue with hers as he moved in and out of her. Lifting his head, he looked down at her.

"When you come, bite me." She looked at him, dazed. "Kerry, I want you to mark me. Bite me and tear into my flesh."

When she nodded, he moved down her throat to her breast and sucked hard, taking as much of her tender flesh into his mouth as he could, when he felt her lick along his shoulder. She was going to do it; she was going to mark him. As soon as her teeth sank into him, he felt his balls release, his cum jettison into her. He bit her as well, tearing his canines into her breast as her own climax screamed from her. Nothing in this world could have prepared him for the love that poured over him from her. Not a single word could have described the incredible feelings he had at that moment. When he dropped onto her, his body spent, her arms fell to her sides and he knew that for as long as he breathed, this woman, above all others, would be his. Rolling to his side, he pulled her with him. She blanketed his body with hers, and he closed his eyes.

They wouldn't be able to stay out there long, as he could feel snow beginning to drift over them. He looked up at the darkening sky. When she lifted her head, he was ready to throw her off him and do battle with whatever had startled her. But she smiled at him.

"Burton Puckett."

Reed smiled back and reached for his brother, the genius. He relayed the information and went to find their basket. When Marc told him that he'd look now that everyone had left his house, Reed detoured around the house to the hot tub just off the deck. There were stairs that went up to their bedroom, so he wasn't worried about going through the house naked. When she was deep in the water and moaning, he laughed.

"You like this? I was actually not sure if I wanted to keep it when I bought the house. Caitlynne and Walker have one, but I don't think I ever saw them use it."

"I'd use this all the time if it were mine." She moaned again and sank down into the water to her shoulders. He reached for her foot. "That feels wonderful."

"Don't you think of this place as yours?" She looked at him oddly. "This house, the furniture, all the things in it, don't you see them as yours too?"

She looked around the decking and then at the house. "I've never really given it any thought, I guess. It's all yours, isn't it?" He shook his head. "Oh. I guess I just assumed it was your house since everyone calls it that."

"It's our house." She sank back into the water, and he waited for her to say something. When she didn't, he pulled her to him. "You don't like this place, we can get another one, one you can help pick out."

"I love this house. It's very you." She looked away. "You're a lot different than me, Reed. I have nothing but what I have in that little case upstairs. I've never lived in anything my entire life but rentals and apartments. I've owned things, but.... What I'm trying to say is, I don't know what to think of this house. I'm not even sure what to do in this house."

"Whatever you want. If you want to redecorate, I'm fine with that. I've invested well. I have a good job that I love. I have more money than I can spend in a lifetime. But this house is just that, a house. You're my home. You make me want to come home nightly and be a better man." He reached for the small box he'd put behind the towels. "I'd very much like for you to be my wife. Will you marry me, Kerry Stephens?"

"Oh my." He slipped the ring on her finger and watched her face as she looked at it. "It's very beautiful."

"My dad helped me pick it out. He was with me and irritated me to the point I wanted to choke him, but he said this one was perfect. I had to agree when I saw it." She held it up to the moonlight, and they watched it twinkle along the water. He cleared his throat. "Is that a yes?"

She grinned at him. "I think so, if you're sure. I think you're making the biggest mistake of your life, but I love you and want to be your wife."

"I accept."

~~~

The kitchen phone was ringing when they walked in the next morning. Kerry looked at Camps when he answered. Then when he turned to her, she sat down. This couldn't be good.

"Thank goodness. I've just woke up and there is blood everywhere." She tried to think who it was when she realized it was her father...Norman. "She's bleeding too. I think he might have killed her."

"Who's bleeding? And who killed her?" She saw Camps leave the room but didn't care. "What's going on there? I swear to you if this is another of your lame attempts to get money off me, I'll — "

"I called an ambulance and they won't come here. They said that the hospital won't take her either because of outstanding bills. My daughter is dying because you were too tight-fisted to give us the money when we wanted it." She looked up when Reed knelt in front of her. She adjusted the phone so they could both hear.

"I'm not sure what you're talking about. Tell me again. What's going on and when did it happen?"

"Sometime last night I got up to use the facilities. When I was coming back through the living room, I saw a shadow. When I called out and no one answered, I moved forward to see what it was, and someone hit me. I think it was Death. He and your sister were arguing yesterday evening, and now this." She had a feeling that they always argued and liked it, but Norman continued. "I think he hit me. Yes, that's it. He did. I struggled with him for a time, and I must have knocked his cell phone from his body. That's what I'm calling you on, because you didn't pay the phone bill and they've shut that off as well. You know you're very ungrateful. I've given you love and support all these years, and this is how you repay me? Ungrateful, I tell you again."

She looked at Reed, who was pulling out his own cell phone. She tried to think what to do when she heard her sister moan. She started to tell him she'd be right there when something occurred to her.

"You say you struggled with Gilbert?" He asked her who that was. "Death, his real name is Gilbert Baker. How did you struggle with him?"

"What on earth does that have to do with what's happening? Your sister is hurt again and again. It's all because of you. You'll have to come here and get us and take her to the hospital. I'll just suffer through my injuries because of hers." That didn't sound right to her either.

"You've never struggled with anyone in your life, not unless it benefited you in some way. And if Death hit her, she more than likely deserved it. So do you, for that matter." She heard him sputter and looked at Reed, who was looking at her, shocked. "And another thing, paying your bills is not my responsibility. It never was and it never will be. Call an ambulance and tell them you think she's dying, which I highly doubt, and see if they don't come. And as for the hospital, you should really check more if you're going to come up with a story. I paid those bills off months ago. And I know she's not been back, because they're supposed to okay it with me before I let them bill me. Which you should know is not going to happen again."

He started to say something else, but she'd had enough. Taking the phone to the cradle, she slammed it down and stood there and counted to ten. Then she counted again. When she turned around, she looked at Camps and Reed.

"I'm hungry. Do you think we could have a big breakfast before you go to work?" Camps nodded, and she looked at Reed. "It was a trap. I don't know how I know that, but it was. Norman was trying to get me to the house."

He nodded, and she sat down again. "Are you all right? You did a great job. I've never been prouder of anyone in my life."

"Myself as well, mistress." Camps handed her a glass of tea. "Drink it down now before you settle. The sweetness will do you good. And I've steak if you'd like too. Bacon, sausage…. You know, this calls for the works. Have a seat, Mr. Reed, and I'll have you a large breakfast in no time."

By the time they were sitting down to eat after helping put things together, Khan and Monica had shown up. They'd brought the twins, who were just starting to walk. They walked between the adults while they ate, getting treats from all of them. Kerry picked up little Abby and sat her on her lap when Khan brought up Burton.

"He's a collector, like you said. And as far as we can tell, that's about all. He does have some dealings with a few other people, but not now." He looked at Monica before he continued. "My wife has an idea. I don't hate it, but I don't care for it either."

"He just doesn't like it because it wasn't his idea. And his mom thinks it brilliant. Caitlynne thinks it'll work too." Kerry looked between the two of them and realized that they really loved each other. Monica smiled at her.

"I'm sorry. I just wanted to tell you thank you." Khan looked at her and smiled. "You guys make me realize that there is goodness in this world. That's all."

"Thank you...what's that?" Monica grabbed her hand. "Holy shit, Reed, that's beautiful."

Abby started saying, "Shit, shit, shit."

"Ignore her and she'll stop. But when did this happen? I thought you might propose where we could see you do it."

Kerry flushed and felt her face heat to almost molten. When she glanced at Reed, she could see that he thought it was funny. Suddenly, Khan burst out laughing and he slapped his brother on the back.

"In the woods or the hot tub?" Reed mumbled tub and set his brother off in peals of laughter again. "Damn, boy, you didn't waste any time. Congratulations to you both, and welcome to the family."

"What's the plan, Khan? And leave her alone."

Camps winked at her and handed her another glass of tea while Reed tried twice more to get Khan to shut up. She'd never been so embarrassed in her life.

"Mom is going to lend you one of her eggs. She said if anything happens to it, she's taking it out of your hide. I think this part needs more tweaking, but basically Kerry here calls up this Puckett fellow and tells him she needs some money. She meets up with him and Marc's wife Jonny, who does her stuff. She'll let us know if the guy is in with Gilbert, and if so, what his plan is."

"I can't take one of your mom's eggs. And if it did get broken or even chipped, it would be worthless. No, I don't think so. If we do this, then we use a fake one."

Khan shook his head, but Reed spoke. "He'll know it's a fake in a minute. You said he was a collector. Collectors can spot a forgery a mile away. We have to use the real thing or he'll know something is wrong."

She looked at Camps when he answered the phone, but didn't really pay any attention because she was trying to wrap her mind around using one of Corrine's eggs.

"I've never even seen her collection. Is there something…smallish? Maybe something that is already damaged?" Both men shook their head. "How much is the least expensive one she has? Do you know?"

"I know how much Dad paid for it. Does that help?" She shook her head at Khan. "I have a picture. Would that help you?"

"I'm not sure I want to see it. I love them, and if I see this one, I might just cry. Do you have any idea how much one of them can go for? How hard they are to find?"

"Mom told me." Khan handed her the phone, and she looked at the picture. "She said Dad got it for her as a wedding gift. Mom said that if you want to bait the hook, you have to have a fat worm to do it. Stupid saying, but I think she's right. Do you know this one?"

She nodded. "This one is part of the Imperial eggs. And I would bet one of the originals. Peter Carl Faberge only made a few, about seventy-five, between 1885 until 1917. He gave most of them to the Russian Czars Alexander the third and Nicholas the second as Easter gifts for their wives. I'm betting this one, when opened, has a golden hen inside." Khan nodded. "This is very rare, and worth more than fifteen million dollars. How much did he pay for it, if you don't mind me asking?"

"Dad can talk a man out of his last meal, and this guy, some traveler, told him that he'd found it in a house when he'd been visiting his lady friend in Russia. Dad said the man was down on his luck and that he needed to get back there. Since he was getting married a few months later, Dad said he'd buy it. It's what started Mom collecting them." Khan showed her another picture, this one with the egg open and the hen sitting next to it. "He gave the man two hundred dollars."

"Christ." She looked at Reed and laughed at him. "Hell, we used to play with that damned thing. Mom would be gone doing something and we'd play with the chicken to add to our farm."

"Well then, that settles it. If it can stand you six, then it can withstand me." At least she hoped so.

CHAPTER 13

"My name is Kerry Stephens, and I was wondering if I could set up an appointment with Mr. Puckett. I have something I'd like to see if he wants to purchase." Caitlynne nodded at Kerry, and Reed held his breath. The more they got into this thing, the more terrified he'd become.

Just last night they'd gotten another call from Norman. He was a lot less nice, not that he'd ever been, but over the phone he'd been vicious and ruthless. He'd spewed things at Kerry for so long she'd simply hung up the phone and went to the kitchen. Reed called him back immediately.

"What the fuck is your problem?" Norman had sputtered about Kerry being ungrateful again and that she owed him. "She has paid whatever debt you think she owes you long ago. She owes you nothing."

"I'm her father, and I will say what she owes me. You put her back on this phone this minute or—"

"Or what? You think you can threaten me? Bring it on, you motherfucker. You don't have the resources or the balls to take me on and even hope to win." Norman started to speak again, but Reed had had enough. "You call here again and I will have you arrested for harassment. And trust me when I tell you, I've got more pull than you will ever hope to have."

"She'll come to me and bring money, or her sister and I will be killed. He wasn't happy when the last plan didn't work." Reed glanced at the kitchen door, glad now that Kerry had figured it out and not gone. "I need money, and he needs to kidnap her. You'll pay ransom to get her back, right?"

Reed had hung up, then took the phone off the cradle. He'd called his brothers using his cell phone and told them that this was the only way to contact either of them, and then spoke to Caitlynne.

He'd told her the entire conversation, and her mind had begun to work immediately. "I don't think I'd mention this to Kerry just yet. Let me do some digging. If they're planning to kidnap Kerry, they either have some great planner or they're stupider than we first thought."

Reed thought them incredibly stupid and told her so. "But I think you're right. Norman's call here just a few minutes ago upset her to the point of tears. When I called him back, he told me that bullshit."

"I'm looking into this Puckett guy now. Let me get back to you on him and this Baker guy." And she had, nearly two hours later, and Kerry was setting up an appointment to go and see him.

She nodded at Caitlynne and him. "Yes, I can be there then. But can you tell him I'm bringing a friend with me? Yes, that'll be fine. Ten o'clock."

"You're in?" Kerry nodded at him. "Great. Tomorrow at ten then, and we'll—"

"Today at ten. He has an opening, and he wants me to come in at ten." She looked at the egg that Caitlynne had brought with her. "I'm not sure this is a good idea now."

"You'll be fine. Reed is going to carry his weapon, and if anything goes fucked belly up, he'll get you out by shooting every cocksucker in the place, and you can shift and chew some dicks off." They both looked at Caitlynne. "Sorry, a little hormonal right now. Walker and I are having another baby, and this one is fucking me up."

Reed laughed and hugged her, knowing that it would piss off his brother. When Kerry hugged her, he thought of her being pregnant, and realized they'd never talked about it. He decided that when this was over, they were going to talk about a great many things. He looked up at the clock. It was now or never.

"I've set something up at the court house. If we leave now, we'll be set before you go to the meeting." Kerry looked at Caitlynne, then him. "I know I should have cleared it with you, but I thought we'd get married today."

"Should have cleared it with me? I'm pretty sure you should have. When did you set this up?" He told her yesterday. She left the room, and he looked at Caitlynne, who was laughing.

"Do any of you Bowen boys ever do things after talking it over with your mate? I'm wondering, because it doesn't appear so. You'd think with you being the youngest that you'd have learned something from the rest of them, but I'm pretty sure you're as fucked-up macho as the rest of them." He cocked a brow at her. "No, this is me talking and not the hormones. You guys need to take a breath and think with something besides your dicks once in a while, and you might not end up in the dog house so often."

She left after giving him a hug, and he had a thought to check her for weapons first. After she left he sat down in the chair, and jumped up when the door opened from the dining room. It was Kerry.

"Well? Are you just going to sit there or are you going to marry me?" She looked at Camps. "Do you suppose you could have a nice luncheon for when we return? I'd like to invite his family over after. Unless he didn't tell them this was happening today."

"I did."

She glared at him, then looked at Camps again. "Thank you very much. I'm sorry you have to be pressed into making this on such short notice. Or did he tell you as well?"

"No, mistress, this is...." He had to cover his mouth, and even Reed could see the mirth on his face. "This is the first I've heard of it as well. Will you require a cake?"

She looked at him, and then Camps did. Reed decided that from now on he was going to ask her for everything. He was not going to be made to feel this way again.

"A cake would be nice if you have the time." He put out his hand, and she stared at it for a full minute. He wasn't sure she was going to take it. When she did, she looked up at him.

"Do this again and I'll make Caitlynne being hormonal look like child's play, understand?" Camps burst out laughing and had to leave the room. Reed was going to hurt the man when he returned, but he nodded at her.

"I love you." She nodded again, and they went out the door. Yes, sir, he was going to be more upfront with her from now on. Because, as much as he hated to admit it, she scared the shit out of him.

~~~

Burton looked at his clock again. It was still an hour to go and she'd be here. He got up to make sure that everything was in its place, and then went out to check with his secretary, Rowena Winters, again.

"I swear to you, Burton, if you ask me again about the tray, I'm going to brain you with it." He nodded and flushed. He loved this woman to death. She had kept him out of jail several times because she was simply that good, but there were times when he thought she knew him too well.

"I'm on edge." She nodded and handed him a piece of chocolate from her drawer. She knew that it calmed his nerves. "What if she's not receptive to this? What if I'm wrong?"

"Eat the candy and stop second guessing yourself. You're not wrong. You've had her checked out several times over the past six months. You know as well as I do that she's your niece."

He went back to his office and sat down. His niece. His sister's little girl. Well, not little now, but all grown up. He started to pace again and heard Rowena clear her throat. He sat down and thought about the first time he saw Kerry.

She'd answered the door to the house where he'd been instructed to find Death. Burton had been so stunned by how much she looked like his sister that he'd been rendered speechless for several seconds. She smiled then, and he felt as if he'd been given a great and rare gift...a fond memory of his sister as a child. And now she was on her way here.

He looked over at the eggs she'd collected, unable to flip them for a profit once he'd seen her. He was going to give them back to her, and give her whatever she needed in the way of more money. He didn't think it would be that easy, but he was going to try.

"She's here." He nearly told Rowena to send them away, he was so nervous. "She is here with a man who is insisting that he keep his gun. He said if he can't carry, she's not coming up. What do you want to do?"

149

A gun? She needed someone to follow her around with a gun? For some reason that pissed him off. Who would dare hurt what he considered his only family? He looked at Rowena, who only smiled and went to her desk again. He heard her say to send them up.

He was standing by Rowena's desk when the elevator opened. His breath caught when he saw her. Even though it had only been about three years since he'd seen her the last time, he could see the marked difference in her. And the man standing next to her wasn't simply her bodyguard, but someone who was in love with her. And it looked as if she loved him as well.

"Mr. Puckett, I'm Kerry Bowen. We spoke on the phone." He looked at the man and then back at her when she continued. "I have something I'd like to see if you can purchase from me."

Burton led her to his office, and the first thing that she saw were her eggs. When she went to stand next to them, she looked back at the man and he nodded at her. "I don't understand. I was told that you had sold them for the money."

"I think you should have a seat. Both of you please." She shook her head, and the man went to stand next to her. "I'm so sorry for this, but there is more to us than simply me being a buyer of your eggs, Kerry. I'm your uncle. Your mom was my sister."

"I think we might sit after all." The man led her to the chairs and sat next to her, holding her hand. "I'm Reed Bowen. Kerry and I were married today…this morning as a matter of fact."

He stood up to give them both a hug and stopped when Kerry stood up. She walked over to the eggs and touched each of them before she turned to him to say anything.

"She left me with those people? Why did she leave me with those people?" Burton glanced at Reed, then back at her. "You say you're my uncle. Then why the hell did you leave me there if you knew this?"

"I didn't know. I thought that when your mom had died that you, too, had passed on. Your father was so distraught at the time; all I could get out of him was that he had lost you both. Then a few weeks later, I heard that he'd killed himself. I never got anything else from him prior to that." He sat on the corner of his desk and watched her pace. "When I went to collect a payment on the money that I'd lent you for the eggs, because it was supposed to be just a loan, I saw you. You look a great deal like your mom. Her name was Letitia, and I'd always understood that she died giving birth to you. She'd been alone, from what I'd been able to find out. Something about your dad being in jail, or some other business that I've never been able to piece together."

"But you found out differently since then." He nodded at Reed as the young man continued. "She died later. We believe at the hand of the man who ended up abusing Kerry. Her father we still can't find, but we have no reason to believe that he's still living. What have you found out?"

"Letitia was killed by Norman Stephens; that much I'm fairly certain of. Her father, at last findings from the PI that I hired, is alive. He does, however, keep to himself and stays out of trouble. He didn't have anything to do with my Letitia's death, but had indeed lost them both. Someone, it appeared, kidnapped them both, and she was told he was dead. His name is Olen, in the event you've not found it."

Reed nodded and went to her and wrapped her in his arms. Burton looked up when Rowena came into his office.

She nodded at them, then stepped out of the office. He excused himself and went to her.

"I know them, the Bowens. Do you?" He nodded. "She's in good hands then. I think that you should tell them everything and be done with it. She's going to have some questions and you have the answers. Give them to her."

He took the chocolate she handed him and went back inside. He'd have to tell them or be as big as a house before this was finished. The woman was forever giving him sweets to keep him calm.

Reed was standing behind Kerry as she had taken her seat again.

"I'm going to tell you some things that are going to seem sort of out there." Burton tried to think how to tell them all the things he knew about her father. "Olen was…he was loving and kind when he wanted to be, which only seemed to be around your mom. But he could…let's just say he had a wildness about him that I hadn't been aware of until later."

"He was a panther." Burton looked up from his notes at the younger man. "So are we. Kerry didn't change until recently, and I'm a pureblood. And we have a little information on her mom, but not a great deal. Perhaps you could fill us in."

"You're a…I never thought that. Christ." Reed sat down, but he didn't say anything more. "I would say prove it, but I'm not sure my heart can take much more. The first time your father changed, it was to leap at me when I'd hugged Letitia to me. She'd just told me that she was pregnant with you. After that…after that, I got the story from them. He changed her before they were wed and she'd been meaning to tell me. How do you not tell someone that?"

"It's against our laws. You said that you no longer think my father was responsible for my mom's death. Why not?" Burton looked at her, his heart breaking for her. "Never mind. I need to know, but now I need to know how you're involved with Gilbert Baker. He's trying to kidnap me and hold me for ransom and having my...the other people I grew up with help him."

"Involved? Not me. The little pisser never has paid me back for the other loans I've spotted him. He has this grand idea that he can—" His heart stopped beating for several seconds. "Mother of Christ, he's going to do it. He's going to actually try and do it."

He shouted for Rowena and asked her to bring in all the transcripts from his conversations with Baker. She hurried out and then came back with a large bag of his favorite kind of chocolate, dark and filled with nuts. He opened the first small bar and popped it into his mouth as he handed them both some of the file he had.

"I usually only record conversations when I'm making a business deal, but Baker never did strike me as the stable type, and he never told the truth when a lie was so much more interesting. Ah, here is it." He started to hand them the conversation from several months ago, but took them to his conference table to spread out. "He was going to buy up this parcel of land from me. I didn't really care, but he seemed to have a real need for it and I was willing to sell it, but only after he paid off the outstanding loans. He even bragged on what he was going to do with it."

"And what was that?" He looked at Kerry and knew that she was supposed to be a big part of the plans that the idiot Baker had started. "I told you he was going to kidnap me. I can only assume that it was to get the money to get his project going."

"He was going to open a hunting range." Reed looked at him sharply. "I think your husband here got it. It was to hunt humans for fun and profit. He had this idea that he could get others like him, wolves and other paranormals, to pay him a great deal of money to hunt and kill humans. He seemed to think that he'd be a millionaire in a very short amount of time."

"That's barbaric." He nodded at Kerry. "And you knew this? You knew the reason he was going to buy the land, and you were going to sell it to him. Why, that makes you no better than—"

"I wasn't. I'm not going to, I swear to you. I've just been leading him on until I could get another buyer. But I told him that if he had the money and paid me off, I would sell, or to another buyer if one came along. I never in all honesty...I never believed he'd do it at all. In this market and with real-estate going to shit, I've not had a great deal of luck. I won't sell to him, not ever. But if not this property, then someone else's." He pushed the last papers in the file at them. "You can see here what the property was worth and what it's worth now. I'm not hurting for the money, so I'll just sit on it forever if need be."

Reed looked them over, then pulled out his cell phone and stepped into the hall, closing the door behind him. He was only gone a minute, two at the most, but when he returned, Burton looked at him. This was going to be wonderful. He just knew it. The man had a perfect poker face, and when he wanted you to see something, you knew it.

"I'll give you fifteen percent over the land value." Burton shook his head, not wanting to sell to them but give it to them if they wanted it. "I can't go any higher than that, but I can get investors if need be. My family is not without funding."

"I know your family, Reed. I've done a great deal of work with you as a corporation. But if you want it, then it's yours. A wedding gift so to speak." Kerry and Reed both shook their heads. "Then I'll sell it off in small plots, and you'll have neighbors around your nice property and you'll not be able to run. I assume that's what you want it for."

"It's near our house now and butts up against the family property too." Burton looked down at where he pointed and laughed. "Yeah, it seems we've been neighbors for a while now."

By the time they left, he'd given them the property and had an address and phone number where he could contact them once this was over. He was also sending Kerry's eggs to her new home. Burton had even looked at the egg she'd brought him.

"I would love to purchase this. I have an eye for the finer things, and this is extraordinary." Reed had laughed and said his mom would kill him, as it was hers to use as bait. But he did get to drool over it for a while.

Burton looked up when Rowena came into his office and took the bag of candies from him.

"You should know that I've had a check done on our Mr. Bowen. Their family is one of the most respected families in the state, not that we didn't already know that. Not to mention the panther community." Burton nodded. "Something else. Reed and his sister-in-law worked for the CIA up until a few months ago. They now run the local police where they live."

He'd known about the police but not the other. "She's in good hands, and when this thing is finished, I'm going to go and tell her about her mom and dad."

"That'll be hard on you both." He nodded, and she stood up. "I guess I'll have to lay in a larger supply of candies then. Could be you'll need to start working out at the gym, too, if this keeps up."

He was still laughing an hour later when his phone rang. It was Reed. Burton heard the sirens in the background as he spoke.

"They've taken her. Her family has taken her, and the motherfucker is going to pay." Burton stood up. "He has my father too. And he's just signed his death certificate."

"What can I do to help?"

CHAPTER 14

Kerry watched her father-in-law as the van they were in seemed about to roll every second. He didn't move, but she was sure he was awake. When he suddenly opened his eyes and winked at her, she nearly cried out with joy. The old buzzard had her scared to death.

"You okay?" She nodded. "Didn't see that one coming a mile off. I figured he'd try to take you, but damn it, did he have to do it with me in the car with you? I could have been instrumental in getting you back and being the hero."

"He hit you so hard." He snorted and put his hand on his head, but there was no blood. "I'm pretty sure he knows you're something different, but I don't think he knows I am."

"He doesn't. Did you hear him say that he hated humans? He was talking about you. Seems to think you're just a plain Jane and he can do whatever he wants to you." He looked at her hard. "He can't, and you won't let him either, understand?"

"Reed said to try and figure out where he's taking us. I can't see anything. Can you?" She'd been trying to get sat up for the past ten minutes, but all she'd managed to do was tighten the bonds around her wrists. She looked at

George and wanted to cry. "He'll pay to get us back, won't he?"

"Course he will, if it comes to that. But we're not going to let it. Corrine said to tell you to buck up or she'll come after you. She can be a mite on the mean side when the mood suits her." Kerry knew he was lying to try to make her laugh, and she appreciated it, but she was terrified. She felt Reed touch her mind.

He's not contacted me as yet to demand a ransom. Have you stopped moving?

Not yet. But your dad is awake now. I think he hit him pretty hard, but he seems to have healed already. He's talking to your mom. She pulled at the bonds at her wrists. *He's got us both tied up. How did he get us when all we were doing was picking up diapers for the baby? I mean, I didn't even know we were going anywhere until George and I were asked to go.*

I don't know, love. Unless he was watching the house to see when and where we might be going. I'm glad about Dad, but if it comes to it, protect him. Mom said he's a bit of a fool when he's in trouble. Jack has some favors she's calling in to find you. Don't be alarmed if other animals come close to you. She has a friend that can be a hawk too.

She has a friend that's a...you know, I don't care. I just want to get away from this idiot Baker. Did I tell you what he called me? A human. As if I couldn't kick his ass before I changed, now it's going to be all out war. He laughed, and she told him to behave. *I want to come home to you. It's our wedding day, and I'm with your dad and this damned wolf that makes me so mad I want to shift into my cat and tear his wolf to pieces.*

Try to refrain from that, because if you shift with your hands tied, it could cause you to sever them. And I want to be with you as well. Do you have any idea the plans I had for your luscious body? The first thing I was going to do to you? He growled

158

low, and her body seemed to catch fire. *You are going to be so sore when I finish with you.*

Christ. I could come now. She felt the van they were in slow. *I think we're going to stop. I can smell some…that's weird.*

What is? She lifted her head and saw that George did the same. She had a feeling he was talking with someone else and figured it was his mate again. When she tried to bring in as much of the scents around her as she could, she realized what she smelled.

I smell our pond, but it's a little different. She tried her best to figure out what it was about it that made it different when it occurred to her. *Remember when we took a bath in the water and we ended up on the far side? You said it was different because of the fact that no one had been there before. You said that all the scents from the animals that moved over our property weren't there. I think we're on that side of the pond.*

Fantastic. I'm on my way. Try to keep safe for me, love, I need you. She told him she needed him as well, and he sent her his love. *When I find you, I'm going to beat your pretty ass, because I'm hard just thinking about it being pink from my touch.*

Find me soon and I'll more than make it worth your while.

He growled again just as the door was being torn open. There in front of her stood Dora and Gilbert. And they didn't look all that happy. She started to move forward when she felt a pain in her head, then nothing at all.

When she came to, she found that she'd been moved to a dark room. When she shifted on the floor, she realized it wasn't a room but a dirt floor. She tried to reach for Reed and hit a hard wall. Waiting for her eyes to adjust, she was shocked to find that she was deep within a cave.

"You should have just let us kidnap you in the first place." She looked toward the voice and saw her sister sitting within a light, and knew that she was near an opening. "This would have gone so much better if you would have just let me have what I wanted, and then you'd be okay and that other man wouldn't be dead."

Dead? George was dead? She tried reaching for him, thinking it would be easy if they were in the same place, but again hit a wall. She tried to think what to do when Dora started talking again.

"You're really stupid if you think that after all this is over I'm not going to bleed you dry. I hate you and the fact that you simply won't do as I tell you. What the hell is wrong with you giving me what I want?"

Kerry ignored her. "Where is he?" Dora shrugged, and Kerry felt her cat stir under her skin. She was tied up with those plastic ties, and remembered what Reed had told her would happen if she tried to shift like this. "You can't possibly think that if you killed their dad any of the Bowens will give you shit, do you? I mean, I know you're stupid, but certainly not that much."

"I'm better than you. At least my mom didn't drop me off on a door step and run off." Kerry started to tell her that her mom didn't drop her anywhere, that Norman had killed her, but she didn't get the chance. "You just wait and see. Death said that he'll give whatever he can, 'cause you're his wife."

"That's enough." Gilbert walked more into the little part of the cave she was in after telling Dora to go and check on the old man. Kerry was so relieved that she nearly told him thanks. At least George wasn't dead.

"What do you hope to gain by this? Money? I'm pretty sure you're going to be shit out of luck." He backhanded her, and her cat snarled at her. He took a step back. "Yeah, you piece of shit, not so easy to slap around now, am I?"

She jerked on her hands and felt the ties bite into her skin. She was going to kill this man if it was the last thing she did. He didn't come any closer to her, but she could feel not only his rage at her but confusion as well.

"You mated with that bastard, and he changed you." She shook her head, and he started toward her. "You weren't a cat before. I would have noticed it. Norman said that your mother said you'd never shift, that you didn't have the right genes. And now you're mated to that fucking panther? What the fuck, Kerry, didn't you know I had big plans for you?"

"I'm sure you did, but I've always been a cat, you moronic dick. She just didn't want to come out and play until the right man helped me." She felt his rage boil over, and then he shifted. She watched as he circled around her several times before he lay down. "You think you scare me? You don't, not any more. Why don't you cut me loose, you fucking prick, and let me show you just how much you don't frighten me anymore?"

He snarled at her, and she growled back. She was pretty sure he was bigger, but she had hatred on her side. When he crawled on his belly closer to her, she let just enough of her cat go to snap at him, and he leapt back. Yeah, she was bad ass.

The leap startled her, and all she could do was put up her hands to protect her face. When she fell backwards her head exploded in pain, and she tried to hold on and fight the blackness. But when he hit her again, this time ramming his body into hers, she knew she wasn't going to win this battle.

~~~

Reed was exhausted. His body ached in places he never knew existed. Lying down, he let his cat rest. He had to find his mate.

You need to try and rest a little. What sort of good do you think you're going to do her if you're dead on your feet? Reed looked at Khan when his cat lay down beside him, clearly as tired as he was. *Mom is frantic, but she's putting together a huge dinner to bring out here for us. Camps said to tell you that he had faith that you'd bring his mistress home.*

I hope so. It had been twelve hours since she'd contacted him that she'd been taken, and six since they'd been searching the area around the pond on all sides. Neither her scent nor that of his dad were there. He looked up when he heard a stick break nearby, and nearly jumped at the woman there, but Khan stopped him.

Let's just follow her for now. She might lead us to them, or to someone that can help us find out where they are. He didn't want to follow Dora. He wanted to jump on her and tear her throat out. Then he smelled it. His dad. Khan must have as well, because he could feel his brother tense up.

Stay close to her and I'm going to go back and see —

Reed cut him off. There was no way Khan was going back to find Reed's mate while Reed followed this bitch.

You follow her. He thought Khan was going to tell him to do what he'd said, but he finally nodded. *I'll contact you if I hear anything.*

See that you do. And you be careful and try not to kill anyone please.

Reed said nothing. He wasn't going to make any promises that he wasn't sure he could keep. When Khan moved in Dora's direction, Reed turned and moved along the path she'd come from.

It didn't take Reed long to find her scent. Once he did, he found several others, but none of his dad and wife. He was wondering how he was going to find them when he got a whiff of something he'd not smelled before. It took him a few minutes to realize it was a panther, and he was very sick.

Reed followed the path up the long steep hill until he came to rock. There were several openings into the mountain this far up, but there was no time to explore them all. He moved along the edges of the larger stones trying to find a scent when he heard someone approaching from behind him. Going to the small stand of trees just on the skirting of the stone, he hid behind a large tree.

It was the panther. And he was more than sick; Reed could tell he was dying. The way he was breathing and staggering along the path led him to believe that the man didn't have long to live. When the man sat down on a large protruding stone and pulled out a bottle, even from as far away as he was, Reed could smell the liquor.

He had to get around him. When he looked up the mountain, he saw a movement and moved slowly out from behind the tree to go there when the man spoke. Reed felt the hair on the back of his neck dance down his spine.

"You'll find her well enough, but your dad is hurt." Reed didn't move as the man continued. "I would have helped them, but I don't know what I could have done except to have gotten everyone killed, and no way for me to come out here and find someone looking for them."

Reed moved out from behind the tree a little, and the man turned to look at him. There was something familiar about him that made Reed step more out into the open area. The man scooted around on the stone so that he was facing him.

"I can hear you if you would let me." Reed nodded once, and the man put out his hand. The closer Reed got to him the more he could smell something else beside the sickness. The man was panther all right, but he smelled of

163

Kerry. Faintly, but he could smell her on the man. Reed rubbed his head under the extended hand and felt the man's finger curl into his fur and touch him deeper. There was no malice in the gesture, but it did deepen their connection.

Who are you and what are you doing up here? You're panther; that much I know, so how the hell did you get this ill? Reed looked up the mountain again. *I need to go soon. Tell me what you know. Please?*

"I'm Olen Hendricks. And I can see by the look on your face that you've heard of me." Reed nodded. "Good. I didn't want to have to explain what I am to you. Do you love her?"

The change in subject was abrupt, but Reed had been working with Caitlynne for so long that he was an expert at keeping up. The woman could change the subject five times in a single sentence and expect you to keep up.

I...I do actually. I didn't realize how very much until just now.

Olen nodded and looked to his left. Reed felt his brother, Walker, coming toward him.

"You'll need them all. Your family, I mean. I know about where he's taken her, but I'm not positive once you get inside the cave. I know it's deep and has more twists and turns than a pig's tail, but you'll find her."

Reed reached for his family and asked them to come to him.

Why does everyone think you're dead? The man lowered his head, and Reed didn't think he was going to answer him. *I won't tell her you're alive if you don't want me to, but I think she'd want to know.*

"I let them inject me with all kinds of drugs to kill me off. Some of them made me sick; others did nothing at all.

164

Then one day they brought me into this padded room and said I was going to die, that something they gave me stuck." He snorted. "Stuck. Like they put a bandage on me and now they found a way for it to stay there. But they were right, I'm dying. Got some sort of untreatable thing that will take me out in a few months. Less if I can help it."

Reed felt the rest of them coming toward him. Olen watched as they came out of the woods and sat nearby. Olen smiled and looked at Khan before he turned back to Reed. The man looked defeated now.

"I didn't die because I was a coward. The bullet only did some damage, which my cat took care of before I could bleed to death. I knew that my daughter was alive, that Letitia had taken her somewhere safe, and it's taken me all this time to find out where. I didn't kill her. My mate, I didn't kill her like Burton and the others think. The man responsible for that is up there in that mountain. The man who raised her. He beat my Letitia to death with a bat and then buried her in the back of his yard. Tell Burton that for me. Tell him I tried to save her but...but I failed them both."

"You said you lost them both. You told Burton that. What did you mean if you knew that she'd taken Kerry somewhere else?" Reed knew at that moment Olen had no idea what his daughter's name was. Right now he needed to find her, but felt that if he didn't get this information now it would be lost to them all.

"Letitia was human when I met her, and set to marry this other man...Stephens's half-brother. He was as cruel and sadistic as that one up there. When our daughter was born, she was...we knew that she was going to be panther. And when Damien found out, he went nuts. Not about her being a panther, but that Letitia had gotten pregnant. I had her run to hide from him. I thought...Christ, I thought she'd be safer."

Reed looked at Khan when he stood up.

Someone is coming. Wolf. They scattered to hide but watched as Gilbert came into view.

"Who the hell are you and what the fuck are you doing on my mountain?" Reed watched as Olen seemed to shrink into his sickness a little more. "Answer me, old man. What are you doing up here uninvited?"

"Walking around, that's all. I'm dying and wanted to see the view once more before I died." Olen lifted his head to the sky and inhaled deeply. "Have you ever smelled anything this amazing?"

"What the fuck are you talking about? Smell what? All I can smell is you, and you fucking stink." Olen stood up, and Gilbert took a step back. "You need to get your ass gone now."

"Yes, of course." Olen stumbled a little and fell against the wolf. He apologized several times as he backed away. As Olen stepped by Reed and the rest of his family, he dropped something. While he watched him stagger down the hill, Khan laughed.

He's helped us. Reed looked down at where his brother was nodding. *Seems he's helped all of us if that's silver I smell.*

The gun lay in the dirt between them, and Reed knew that the stumble had been deliberate. He looked to where the old panther had gone and saw nothing but trees. Reed looked at Khan.

He said she was in one of the caves beyond. He said that he knew Dad was hurt but that Kerry was okay. We have to go up there and get them. Now. They both watched Gilbert as he stood there for several seconds before he, too, moved down the mountain. Reed moved out from the dense woods and made his way upward. He knew without looking that his family was right behind him.

CHAPTER 15

Kerry lay there for several hours before she decided enough was enough. She tried to think how she could get the bonds off her wrist and ankles without a knife. When she thought about her cat, she purred along her skin and made her feel somewhat comforted.

"You want to help me, then why don't you think of a way for us to get the fuck out of this mess?" She purred louder, and the hum was vibrating along her skin. "Listen, we can't just sit here all day. I have to pee really bad, and I don't think the stupid prick is going to let me go long enough to take care of business and kill him. So let's put our minds together and think."

"Who are you talking to? Yourself?" Norman came into the deep cave and sat a few feet from her. "You should know that people think you're insane if you do that."

He laughed, and she wanted to get up and rip his throat out. Her cat seemed to think the same thing. Norman leaned back against the cave wall and looked at her.

"So, you're not speaking to me, are you? That's fine. I have plenty to say to you before Death gets back." He pulled out a small notepad. "I made myself notes so I wouldn't forget anything."

His laughter grated on her last nerve. He didn't so much laugh as he brayed like a jackass. Kind of appropriate if you thought about it, but she doubted he'd find the humor in her calling him a braying jackass. He took out a pencil and licked the tip. She'd only seen people do that on the television, and wondered if he'd seen it too and thought it cool. Stupid man.

"The first thing I want to tell you is that as soon as this is over, you're dead. I don't mind that fact as much as you might think. You've been a pain in my ass for decades and I'm done with you. The money we're going to get from your kidnapping will be more than enough for me to live for a long time." She wondered about Dora, but he answered that for her as well. "Death is about to make us less than three. Oh my, what a grand joke I've just made. Death will visit your sister. I'm just too funny for my own good."

"Why?" Kerry hadn't meant to ask, but it was out before she could stop it. "Why did you do this to me?"

He shrugged. "Why not? You were at the right place at the wrong time I guess. So was that mother of yours. She served her purpose well enough, I guess. Her dying like she did and leaving you to me helped me out a great deal over the years since. Then, when she told me that you were nothing but a human like she'd been before she met your dad, I realized I had no use for either of you. But you did finally come into your own, got a job, and supported us, which I think is only right since I saved you from living in a trash can or even a deep hole with your mom. And now this. You're going to make us very rich."

"This has always been about money, hasn't it? If there wasn't enough money in your pocket, then you simply couldn't make it in this world. Do you have any idea how many dreams I had to give up on in order to keep the two of you happy?"

He laughed. "Do you really think I care what you had to sacrifice? You were nothing to me, Kerry. Not a damned thing. Then you had to become selfish and demanding. Why did you have to change things for us? Dora and I were very happy with the arrangements." He looked at his notes again. "You also should know that the old man you were with is going to die too if he hasn't already. He's in a bit of pain right now."

Kerry wanted to ask if he was tied up as well but didn't. She would bet anything that they'd done it, even to the point of hurting him more to do so. She started to say something about his list when she heard a faint sound through the door that seemed to lead upward.

"You should know something before you go on with your useless list." He looked up at her when she didn't continue. "I'm going to take great pleasure in killing you slowly and with no kind of mercy."

He must have seen something in her face because he looked terrified. She smiled then, a small smile that she knew didn't reach her eyes. Anger seemed to make her cat happy as well, and she let just enough of her go so that her tormentor could see her. When he stood up, she watched him back away quickly.

"That's not possible." She cocked a brow at him incredulously. "She said that you were human. Because she was pregnant with you before she was turned, you couldn't be carrying the gene."

"I'm thinking she might have lied to you to save me. Imagine that. Someone lying for the good of another." An idea popped into her head, and she let her cat go again and felt her canines drop. She bit into the plastic and tore it from her wrists. She was pulling off the one around her ankles when a low growl had her looking toward the door.

George didn't look injured, but she could smell it on him. He was weak and seemed smaller than his usual self. She wanted to go to him, but he stood there looking at Norman as if he was a tasty meal. The fur along George's back stood up when Norman backed up. Kerry laughed.

"I wouldn't if I were you. I'm pretty sure that if you run, he'll enjoy this so much better. And if you don't...." She let the statement hang out there, and Norman looked at her.

"If I don't what? What will he do if I don't run? Surely you don't mean to let him kill me? I'm your father, for Christ's sake." She shook her head. "Thank God. I thought for a minute there you were as heartless as—"

"You misunderstood me. I didn't say I was going to stop him. I meant you're not my father. You and I both know that. And if he wants to run you down and tear your throat out, the only reason I'd be upset with him is because I didn't get to do it." She stood up and reached for the cold wall as all the blood rushed to parts of her body that had been idle for so long. "You're going to help us get out of here, or so help me, we'll both tear you apart."

"I can't do that. Death will come back here and kill me." She only snickered at him, wondering if he was that stupid. "You'll just have to hurt me a little, so he thinks you overpowered me."

I don't have it in me, love, to attack him. You just keep him talking and I'll get some back, but right now, it's all I can do to stand here looking all bad assed. She glanced at George when he spoke to her. *He's a mite stupid, isn't he?*

A lot stupid. She looked at Norman, who was muttering to himself about her being so ungrateful. *Sit down and let him see your canines. That should do the trick of him thinking you're still all that. And, George, I am going to hurt him badly for touching my family. You just watch and see. But you have to stay there. You're not going to die while I'm around. Corrine will kill me.*

George didn't sit but lay down. He growled low when Norman took a hasty step toward him, and he backed up. Kerry had to bite her lip to keep from laughing out loud. Even hurt like he was, George cut an imposing figure.

"All right, I'll help you, but I want something in return. I want money. After Death kills Dora, I'll not have anyone to depend on to do all the things you did for me. I need to have compensation."

"No." He nodded, then looked at her as if he couldn't believe she'd said that word to him. "You'll help or die. I don't really care which you choose, but those are the only choices you're going to get. Not that you won't more than likely get killed later, but for now, that's all you get."

He drew back his hand as if he might come at her and hit her, but George stood up again, and he took a step forward. That's when she saw the large stone lodged in his furred chest. Christ, it was bleeding profusely, too.

You need to stay put before you bleed to death. What the hell is wrong with you running around like you're invincible or something? Are all you Bowen men this stubborn?

We are. But I wouldn't say you're all that sweet as pie either, young lady. He lay back down, and she could see what the move had cost him. *I'm not sure, darling, but I don't think I'm going to make it. You might have to save us both. I'm feeling a mite tired. Will you tell my love that I tried my best to make it back to her? She's a wonder, that woman, for putting up with me all these years. Tell her that I'm so sorry and that I love her with all my heart and then some.*

Don't you dare die on me, old man. I will kick your ass if you even think that again. He snorted at her but didn't answer. *George Bowen, what would Corrine say to you if she knew that you'd given up? Please don't do this. Just stay back and out of the way. I've got this. When I kill his sorry ass, I'll get us help. You have to hang on. Please just stay back.*

She'll be pissed at me. And you know that I can't stay out of it. Gotta keep my fingers in the pie, so to speak. He yawned. *I'll hang on here, but could you shut him up? I've never seen a man so bent on emptying his head through his mouth before. What the hell is he talking about?*

Kerry turned back to Norman and listened. "Shouldn't have let her live. Had I just killed her off, none of this would be a problem. Yes, sir, a problem is what I have here. A dead wife, a panther in my family. Well, not my family, but.... Dead all the same, she is. I should have taken her out years ago. Then I'd not have that damned Dora to contend with. Stupid girl would sleep with anything with a dick. Including dogs. No, no, no, he said he was a wolf, not a dog. Must remember that or he'll hurt us again." He looked at her, and she could see the fear and something else in his eyes. "I simply must kill you as well."

He advanced quickly, and something...someone knocked her out of the way. Before she could shift, even if that's what she'd meant to do, Norman lay with his head removed from his shoulders, and George lay not two feet from him, panting and bleeding more.

He was going to kill you, the slimy bastard. And now...now I'm going to die. Tell her...tell Corrine that I love her. He closed his eyes, and she ran to him. When a noise sounded behind her, she shifted and leapt at the same time. It was too late before she realized that Reed had found them.

~~~

Death moved into the house and crept down the hall toward her bedroom. Dora always left the door open, even when they were having sex. He'd often wondered if she wanted someone to watch them. He'd gotten a great deal of pleasure from that. But today for some reason she'd shut the door. No matter. He had a key.

His wolf stirred along his body in anticipation of the kill. He touched the doorknob when he heard something behind him, and moved back into the room next to hers. Dora was coming down the hall with a plate and a cup in her hand. Good, this was going to be over very quickly. When she touched the door handle, he reached out and grabbed her around the throat.

"You're a royal pain in the ass. I'm going to take pleasure in killing you." He pressed his hand over her mouth when she opened it to scream. "No, I don't think so. Not that anyone would hear you, but I just don't want to hear it."

He took her into the bedroom, holding her body tightly against his. There was no reason for this opportunity to go to waste, and he threw her onto the bed. She tried to scramble away, but he grabbed her leg and started to tear away her pants.

"Don't do this. I love you, Death. Please don't kill me." He ripped her clothes off until she lay there, naked. His cock jumped at the thought of fucking her while she tried to get away. "I'll do what you want, even suck you off first."

He liked that idea and let her go. She moved to the edge of the bed and then stood up. Christ, she looked good enough to eat right now. When she dropped before him and unsnapped his pants, he curled his hand into her hair and held her to him. She freed his cock, and he nearly came all over her when she fisted him.

"Suck me until I come down your throat." She nodded and wrapped her hair around him. "Stop fucking around and suck me."

Her mouth was hot and wet. He rocked his hips into her heat and felt her hand cup his balls. He put both his hands around the back of her head and held her while he fucked her hard. He was going to come down her throat and break her neck at the same time. As soon as the thought entered his mind, he felt a sharp pain near his balls. Then, when a second, more pronounced pain ripped through him, he pulled back from Dora's mouth and looked down at her.

Her mouth and face were covered in blood. He staggered back again, just realizing that he was hurting really badly now. Looking down at his body, he cried out when he saw what she'd done to him.

"You told me that one." He looked at her and she smiled, licking the blood from her fingers. "You told me that silver would kill you, and I might not have done it if you hadn't threatened me. So now...." She shrugged as he fell back against the wall.

There were three long spikes sticking from him, two in his upper-thigh and one in his dick. He reached down to pull them from him when she laughed. His wolf snarled at him and he wanted to shift, but knew that he couldn't with the silver racing through his body.

Pulling the first one free, he held his cock while blood poured from him in long rivers of red. The second one, the one closet to his hip, pulled free easily enough, but the third one was not coming loose. She had hit bone.

"Why?" He dropped to his knees, too weak to do anything else. "Why the fuck would you kill me like this?"

Her laughter again made him look up. She held a gun in her hand, and she was pointing it right at him. She smiled at him, showing her teeth, and he wasn't really surprised to see that they were stained with his blood.

"Because I can." She sat on the bed to continue speaking as he weakened more. "I just didn't think it would take this long. I thought...I don't know, that you'd blow up or something. I didn't know you'd just bleed to death."

He pulled out the final piece of silver and staggered back to his ass. Pain raced over him, and he felt his wolf snarl at him again. This wasn't good. He was dying, and they both knew it. He was going to shift to try to save them both, but wasn't sure that he could do it and kill her before the silver she had in her gun would do its worst.

He let the wolf take him and felt the bullet enter his chest. Reaching out to her, he ripped at her throat with his claws and felt the satisfying tear of her flesh, heard the scream that came from her injured vocal cords, and felt hot, fresh blood splash across his muzzle and face. They both tumbled back onto the floor even as she fired again and again. Each time a bullet entered him, his wolf tore more and more at her. Death knew the exact moment that she was dead and lifted his head, heavy with his own death, to look down at the horror that he'd done to her.

Her throat was torn to shreds; he'd nearly torn her head off. Her face, once pretty but not beautiful, now held a macabre appeal to him that he found lovely and sexy. Letting his wolf have his way, he licked along her ravaged cheek and tasted still warm blood, and threw back his head and howled. Moving off her completely, he looked at the rest of her.

Her gut was open and intestines spilled to the floor and over the blankets that had been ripped from the bed. Her legs fared no better in that Death's wolf had clawed at them severely and opened muscle to the bone, and broken them in several places. She had gotten what she deserved. Then he looked down at his own body.

Blood poured from his chest, belly, and leg. She'd shot him a total of five times, so many that he could hardly tell one wound from the next, they had done such damage. As his body weakened, he let his wolf go and took his human form, knowing that when they were found—and they would be soon if the sirens were any indication—they'd have no idea what had happened here. Laughing slightly, he was glad now that he'd taken the time to ensure that his dream came to fruition. That there was at least someone now that would carry on his idea of a hunting ground for humans. His friend the vampire was going to buy the property from Puckett and call it Natural Habitat.

Dean had been his friend for years and now the man would be rich. He'd take the money and use it just as he'd told him to do. It had been Dean's idea to visit Dora that first time and make her afraid of him; they'd laughed about it for hours afterwards. Now all that was a moot point as Dora was going to be dead long before the deal went through. But then so was he.

Death coughed once and felt the blood pour from his mouth. This was taking longer than he'd thought. His wolf tried to heal them, but there was no hope for it. Even he had to know that. When the door burst open at the front of the house, he heard the person shout that he was the police, to stand down. Laughing again, he thought that was all he could do at this point. When the officer came into the room, he took a hasty step back and nearly fell in all the blood.

"What the fuck?" Death couldn't have agreed more with his statement and closed his eyes. Smiling, he wondered if they would blame Norman for all this. He hoped that when the panthers found Kerry and the man, that Dean would tear them apart as Death had done to Norman's daughter. Death finally let his namesake take him and felt the relief of no longer being in pain.

CHAPTER 16

Corrine sat in her chair, where she'd been for several days now. She'd watched the boys and their wives come and go, but she just didn't have the energy to speak. Her mate was gone. She glanced up when someone said her name, but she didn't have any interest in the food tray. She hadn't any need for it. When Monica sat it in front of her on the little table, Corrine looked away. It sickened her.

"I miss you." Corrine didn't even acknowledge her. "I've been trying and trying for days now to figure out how to bring you back to us, but I don't think you want to come back. I think you would be happy if we let you starve and die. I'm sorry, but I really don't think I can do that."

"I've lost everything." She hadn't realized her voice could sound so full of hurt and sorrow until then. "He's all I had in the world for so long, and now he's gone."

"Yes. He's gone, but you're not." Corrine just wanted them all to leave her alone. She decided that today she'd go back to their home...her home now...and let things go as she wanted.

Monica left a few minutes later, and one of the other girls came in. Corrine didn't really care who it was, but knew when she spoke this was the one she most did not want to speak to. Because of her, she was all alone.

"He spoke of you while he lay there. His last thoughts were of you." Corrine glanced at Kerry, then away. "He saved my life, but I can't save yours in return, can I?"

"I don't want you here." The words spilled out before she could think. "I would prefer to be left alone by all of — "

"No, I'm pretty sure you had it right the first time. You don't want *me* here. And believe it or not, if I could do it all over, I would have gladly taken his place." Corrine looked up when she stood, feeling the shadow fall over her. "I'm really sorry, Mrs. Bowen. More than you'll ever believe me to be. I've just come here now to tell you goodbye."

It took a few seconds for what she said to register in her mind, but when Corrine looked around, Kerry was gone, as was the tray. She wondered what she'd meant, and decided that finally someone was going to give into her wishes and leave her be.

Corrine had never loved anyone like she had her George. He'd been a pain in her bottom for decades, made her so mad she wanted to clobber him, but he'd also made her smile. He'd made her laugh when she was too upset or blind to see that there was humor in a great many things. She simply didn't want to live without him beside her.

Khan sat down across from her, and she sighed. Wouldn't they just leave her alone?

"I'm taking you back to your home in the morning. I know that's where you want to be so…Monica said that you needed to be there, so we've all agreed to let you do what you want. Then when the funeral is over for the others, we'll see about getting things as back to normal as we can. I'm going to miss them." She nodded, happy that she could live out her days in peace.

"You've all grown now. I'm happy for you all." He nodded and looked out the window that she'd been staring out for so long. She looked too, and saw Reed and that woman near a car. "She will give him children, I think."

"She will, I suppose. I'm glad they'll get a fresh start." Khan left her to herself, and she watched her youngest son hug his wife and her get into a car. When he moved to the woods after the limo pulled away, she wondered what was happening, but honestly didn't really care. She was going home.

Corrine must have dozed off, because when she woke up, it was dark in the room. There was a small light in the hall, but the room she was in was dark as pitch. Standing to use the bathroom, she had to grab onto the back of the chair, she was so dizzy.

Moving slowly out into the hall, she realized that the house was quiet and at rest. She could hear the large clock in the hall ticking, as well as the house settling down for the night. She'd been here when word came back to her that George was gone from her, and here she'd been since. But in the morning she'd be where she needed to be most.

To avoid looking in the mirror, she used the toilet and flushed without ever turning on the light. She was headed back to the den when a noise made her turn. Reed was just coming in the house, and he had a large box with him.

"I'm sorry. I thought everyone would be in bed." She shook her head at him. "I'll just put this in Khan's office and be on my way."

Corrine waited for him to return, and when he did, he moved by her and to the door without speaking. She said his name, wondering if he had planned to go without saying more to her.

He spoke to her without turning. "She's gone to DC. I'm headed there now. She...we couldn't bear to be here with you hating her so much, so we've decided to sell out and move back. I've been offered a good job, and I start on Monday."

"Reed, I...." She didn't know what to say to him, and he seemed to know it. He nodded once, moved out of the house, and closed the door quietly behind him. Corrine stood there for several minutes just trying to wrap her mind around what he'd just said. He was leaving?

Corrine started for the door to stop him, to...she wasn't sure what, but she knew that this wasn't right. Before she could touch the doorknob that he'd just closed, Caitlynne spoke softly.

"You've driven them away. I hope you're happy with yourself." She turned, ready to tell her that the woman had killed her mate, when she cut her off. "Oh, I know you're hurting, but I guess you don't care that the rest of us are as well. Little George cried himself to sleep tonight because you ignored him. Abby and little Khan sat with him, not really understanding, but knew that you'd hurt their cousin somehow."

"I'm grieving. Can't you see that? My mate was taken from me. He died because...because of her." She felt her face heat with embarrassment when she realized how loud she'd been. "I can't stand the fact that he's gone from me. I don't want to live any longer knowing that I'll never see him again."

"Good for you." Corrine was startled by her comment, but she continued. "I'm so happy you've got the market cornered on grief and dealing with it. Because in the event you didn't notice, the rest of us are grieving as well. His sons, for one, are torn up about this, but since they've spoken to Kerry, they're not nearly as consumed by it as you've allowed yourself to be."

"You've no right to speak to me that way." Caitlynne laughed. "I don't see the humor in any of this. I've lost my heart."

"No you haven't. You've closed your heart. And that's sadder than his death ever would be." Caitlynne started for the stairs, then turned to her. "She's not coming back here. Not ever. She's told us that Reed may return if he wishes and bring their children if they have any, but she'll never darken the doors to any of our homes again. Kerry didn't kill George, but you're killing her. And for no other reason than you're more dug into what you think happened up there than what really happened there."

"I don't know what you're talking about. She's alive and he's not. What would you expect me to feel? Glad for her? Thrilled that because she'd managed to get herself wrapped up in that family that my mate is dead?" Corrine snorted, her heart breaking for some other reason than George being gone. "She should have made sure he was safe. He was old and not in good shape."

"But he saved her life." Corrine looked at her. "Kerry said that he leapt at Norman and tore his head off him when she'd told him to stay back. She said that he'd told her several times that he was dying, weak from loss of blood, and she'd begged him to…. Never mind. It's too late now."

Corrine went back to sit in her chair. Caitlynne was right. She'd never listened to any of them when they'd tried to talk to her. Not that first day and certainly none after. She'd been grieving, like she'd said, but she'd also been trying to die. Sitting back in the chair, she let the tears fall and thought of her George.

"I miss you. You old fool, what were you thinking getting yourself killed like that?" She felt the air around her stir and looked up at the man standing before her. George. He was back.

"You're a fine one to talk, my dear. Getting myself killed when you're doing nothing but the same to yourself. At least I had a purpose. What do you have in mind?" She sat up, knowing that he wasn't really there but glad he was. "I guess you've nothing to say for yourself then."

"I can join you in the afterlife. Be with you." He shook his head. "What do you mean 'no'? I will most certainly join you. Soon if I can manage it."

"No. If you murder yourself, you've no rights to be with me." He moved to the chair near her and sat back. "She begged me to stay out of it. Told me that you'd be angry with her and with me. I guess she was right, wasn't she? But when that man made to attack her, I knew that I had to do something. She would never have survived had I not done what I did. And then our own baby would have died with her. Would that be what you wanted in order to have me here with you in the flesh? I think you would have done the same."

"I would have done nothing of the sort." But she knew it for the lie that it was, and apparently so did he if his laughter was any sort of indication. "You've left me with nothing."

That brought him up out of the chair. "I've left you with everything. Six fine boys and their lovely wives. Grandchildren to bounce on your knee and tell them about me. I've even left you with my love, all of it, as I've never been able to give it to another and wouldn't have even if I could. You've got more than most have in two lifetimes, and you're throwing it away."

"I need you." She sobbed then and reached out to touch him, and her hand went through him. "You're only a figment of my tired mind. All this isn't real."

"Isn't it, love?" He looked off to his right, and she knew that someone was speaking to him. When he looked back, he looked so terribly sad. "I must go. I won't be able to come back unless you do what's right. And then only to help you along the way."

"You mean get up off my bottom and start to live again?" He nodded. "You'll come for me when I die, when it's my time?"

"Only then." He looked away again and then back at her. "You'll be fine, my dear. Better than fine. But you must move on. You mustn't let the family break up. They'll need each other when the time comes."

He faded away, and she felt the brush of his mouth over hers and smelled him on her. She let the tears flow when he was gone and cried until the sun came up and brightened the room. Lying in her lap was a single yellow rose, her favorite. And when she lifted it to her nose to smell it, she didn't smell the scent of the rose, but that of her mate. And took it to her heart.

"Oh, you old fool, I love you so much."

~~~

Reed was putting the For Sale sign in his yard when Khan's truck pulled up. He tried to ignore him, but when Khan grabbed him up into his bear of a hug, Reed felt the tears he'd been fighting all morning struggle to be let go. He finished with the sign only to have Khan pull it up again.

"You do know that I've listed it with a realtor. And taking this sign out of the ground won't do any good at all." Khan broke the stick over his knee. "Whatever."

Reed started back to the porch to pick up the last of his bags. Kerry had left last night, unable to stand it any longer. He was just leaning over to pick up the bags when Khan spoke.

"The jet is on its way back to get Kerry and bring her home. I've called the realtor and had them take the house off the market. You'll need a place to stay, I think. And Mom is pissed that you think you're leaving."

His heart did a little dance, but he wasn't going to be sucked into whatever fantasy that Khan had dreamed up. His mom hated Kerry, and that was all there was to it. He had to protect her, and this was the only way.

"You should turn on your cell phone so people can call you," Khan said. Reed had turned it off last night before going to bed. Hearing from his family begging them not to go was too much. Khan took his bags.

"Why are you doing this?" Khan nodded to the house, and as much as he didn't want to go inside again, he followed him. "Tell me so that I can get to the airport. The plane is ready to go."

"I told you it's not. It's probably already halfway to DC by now. Kerry isn't aware of what's going on yet, but she will be soon enough. Mom is going to get her." Reed started to go for his truck, to do what he wasn't sure, but his mom was not going to hurt his mate again. "Dad came to visit Mom last night."

Every part of Reed froze. He turned slowly to look at his brother, who had entered the house. He had no choice now but to follow him. This was just too...surreal, he supposed.

"Dad is dead." Khan nodded at him. "Then what do you mean that Dad visited her last night? Last I heard, being dead kind of revoked your visiting rights."

"Be that as it may, she said she talked to him. He told her she was being selfish and mean, basically. He also told her that he loved her and left her a single yellow rose." Reed sat down, trying his best not to look at the rose he'd put in a vase just this morning. "I think he told her to get her ass in gear and live or she'd be on her own in the afterlife."

Reed wasn't sure what to do. Should he tell Khan that his dad had come to him as well? He glanced at the rose and back at Khan. Khan looked at the flower sitting on his empty desk, then back at Reed.

"He was here too?" Reed nodded at Khan. "And what did he say to you? To not sell and stay here with your family?"

"He told me about my son." Reed got up to pace. "He said that he'd be coming by Christmas next year, and that I was to name him after a great man. When I pointed out that his name was taken, he laughed. Laughed like he'd done his whole life."

Khan nodded. "And this great man, did he tell you who he was? I'm betting I can guess. Was it you?"

"Yes. He said that only a great man would protect what was his above all others. Only a great man would stand up for what was right and not run away with his tail between his legs at the first sign of trouble. He told me that leaving here was akin to killing the family."

"It is, but it's not entirely your fault. Mom was...she wasn't handling it well, and you did what any of us would have done. I would have left just to keep the peace, just as you were about to do. But I couldn't stand the fact that just when all of us were going to be home again, you were leaving. I need you here as much as the rest of us do."

"Kerry is hurt." Khan nodded. "I don't know if she'll come back. She said she won't come between us, but she didn't. Mom did."

"She did, but I think...I know that she'll beg Kerry to forgive her. Mom was sobbing when neither of you answered your phones." Reed pulled out his phone and saw that he had nine voicemails, as well as about a dozen text messages. He looked at Khan.

"You think she'll convince her to come back?" Khan laughed. "Yeah, I guess she will. Mom has always been able to make others see her way. But Kerry...Kerry is pretty stubborn too."

"Christ, I hope so. Mom needs to have her ass handed to her on a platter. I've never been so afraid in my life as I was to see her giving up. It was bad enough to lose Dad, but her too?" Reed looked at the flower again. "What else did he tell you? I know you well enough to know by the look you have on your face that there was more. I'm not sure I want to know it, but tell me."

"He said that without family, there was no life, and without life, there was no family." Reed snorted now, but last night he'd been overwhelmed by the words. "He's never been one to wax poetic before. But he's right. I need you guys, but I need her more."

Khan stood up and hugged him again. "Then I suggest you get this house back in order, bring back your cook, and get ready for your wife. I don't think she's going to be too terribly happy when she returns. She'll have spent the better part of three hours with Mom. And that can be scary enough."

Reed sat down after his brother left and looked around. The house had been shut down, cloths placed over furniture that had barely been used. The refrigerator had been emptied, as had the cabinets. All that remained was the car in the garage, which he had planned to sell, as well as his three suitcases. He looked up when he heard someone clear their throat.

"Sir," Camps said softly. "Are we staying or going? Miss Caitlynne was very insistent that you needed me to return, and Miss Ama...she can be quite scary when the mood strikes her, can't she?"

Reed stood up and nodded. "We're staying. And you're right, they're all scary. But I have a feeling that Kerry is going to be livid when she returns. I'm thinking we'll need to come up with something she likes...no, something she *loves* for dinner. Then, my man, I need for you to spend the night elsewhere. I'm going to seduce my wife, and I don't want to worry that we'll embarrass you."

"Very good, sir. I shall stay at home tonight and have a lovely evening with a new book I've only just purchased. It's about a vampire, a man named Aaron MacManus, and his kiss. There are fourteen of them. Will I be needed after all, you think?" Reed nodded. "Very good. Then I will hire a staff so that when the children come, we'll be ready."

Reed was going to work on the children part as soon as humanly possible.

CHAPTER 17

Kerry watched her mother-in-law as she sat across from her, smiling. She wanted to smack that smile right off her face, but was afraid of her. She'd done just what she said she'd do and gotten her on the flipping plane. Her uncle sat next to her. The two of them had ganged up on her when she'd come out of the realtor's office in DC, and had nearly kidnapped her onto this thing.

"You should know that we've also stopped the sale of your house. Reed might not be happy with us either, but we're going to make this work." She glared at Corrine, but said nothing as she continued. "Also, we're having a dinner party on Friday night, one to honor my late husband."

"The one you accused me of killing?" Kerry hated that Corrine had said that to her when she'd come into the house that dreadful night. "I didn't kill him any more than you did."

"I know that. Now."

Kerry was too wrapped up in her own hurt to realize what she'd said at first, and looked at her when said it sank in. "You said it was my fault. You told everyone that would listen that he was dead because of me. I tried to get the old buzzard to back the fuck off, but he wasn't going to have it.

He saved my life, as much as you hate that, but I wouldn't be here but for him."

"I know that too. He told me." Kerry glanced at Uncle Burton, then back at Corrine. "He called on me last night and told me what a fool I was being. He said that I couldn't die or I'd never get to see him in the afterlife. And that I needed…"

"So you decided to come to me and try to make things right. Sorry, but I just don't care if you see him in your afterlife." She felt spiteful for saying that, and knew that she'd hurt her. "Look, I was willing to move away so you'd not have to look at me anymore, for whatever reasons you have in your head. Since you never let me tell you what your mate said to tell you, you'll have to get it from the rest of them. The ones that cared enough to know that I didn't want him to die. I'm going back to DC as soon as this plane lands, and if you try to have me arrested again, I'll…I'll sue you. I need to move on with my life."

"Kerry, I'm so—" She cut her off again, but she wasn't having any of it. "I'm trying to tell you I was wrong, that I'm so sorry."

"So am I." She leaned back in her chair and tried hard not to cry. These people had meant so much to her, and now they…well, Corrine didn't want her in her life any longer. She'd even had a graveside service for Norman and Dora because she didn't want to overshadow the death of a great man. She wished now that she'd never met any of them.

"We still need to speak, you and me." She looked at Uncle Burton. "We've a great deal to discuss about things that were left open. Can we talk before you go back?"

"No, I don't think so. I'm going back as soon as this thing lands, even if I have to walk. Reed was supposed to follow me sometime today. Maybe we can leave together. I'm sure whatever you have to say to me can be said over the phone, or you can come out to visit us." She heard Corrine sob and watched her as she left the large compartment they were in to go back to the back of the plane. "I've hurt her when all I wanted to do was leave her in peace."

The rest of the ride was made in silence. Corrine returned after a bit and sat down, but she didn't try to talk to her again. Kerry tried to reach out to Reed, but he wasn't answering her, and she thought maybe that was for the best as well. She hoped that she had enough money to fly back, because right now she wasn't sure what was going to happen when she landed.

When they got off the plane, she walked to the hangar behind the rest of them. She was still trying to figure out how much it would cost her to get a one way ticket when she saw Khan coming toward them. Instead of joining him when he hugged his mom, she detoured to the bathroom. This was not going to go well.

"Are you coming out of that stall, or do we have to come in there and get you?" She closed her eyes at the sound of Jack's voice. "We can do it, you know. There's enough magic out here now that we can blow this place apart without much effort."

"Way to go, smart ass. I wouldn't come out either if you threatened me." She smiled at Jonny. "Why does everything have to be do or die with you? Can't you just simply say, 'We'd like to talk to you...can you get done peeing so we can?' Doesn't that sound better than 'Come out or we blow the place up'?"

"I didn't say that. I was simply pointing out that we could if—"

195

Someone cleared their throat, and she knew it was Ama.

"Let's begin again, shall we?"

Kerry heard them say something low, and nearly laughed when Monica called someone a mouthy bitch. Something she thought would describe all of them.

"Get your ass out here now." As Monica was her alpha, Kerry couldn't ignore the command coming from Monica even if she wanted to. She just knew that they weren't going away until they said their piece, and she wanted to get moving.

"Hey, why did you get to do that and I couldn't?" Kerry looked at Jack when she huffed. "I could have ordered."

"You threatened. See how much better my way worked? Now, we're going to leave here and head for the closest bar and settle this thing." They all turned as one to the door, but she didn't move. Monica turned to look at her.

"I'm not going to be talked into anything. I'm going back." Monica shook her head at her. "Yes I am. And short of shooting me, I'm not going to sit with you so you can convince me I overreacted."

"You didn't. Overreact, I mean. She did. And while I can see where you could be hurt, extremely hurt as a matter of fact, it doesn't change the fact that she's your husband's mom." Monica asked the others to leave, and each of them hugged Kerry before stepping out. "You can go if you want, but I can assure you that once you do, Reed will never return. I know you said that he could and bring the babies, but he won't. Khan said that he wouldn't if it was him. Not without me."

"I didn't kill him." Monica took her into her arms as she cried. Kerry had been fighting the tears for so long that once they started to flow, there was no stopping them. She was nearly spent when she felt another set of arms around her and turned to see Reed. Monica left them when Kerry went to his arms.

"I've been out there waiting for you to come out. When I felt you crying, I couldn't wait any longer." She nodded and took the wad of toilet paper he handed her. "I don't suppose you want to go back to the house with me?"

She didn't but said nothing. Kerry wanted him right now and licked his throat. He moaned and tilted his head back more for her. They were nearly to the point of her throwing him to the floor and having him right there. Kerry looked up at him when her cat stirred hard against her skin.

"You're in heat. I can smell it." He leaned down and took her mouth hungrily, and she answered in kind. "I want you. Christ, you're making me hard as stone."

He rocked into her and she moved her hand down to his cock and cupped him. When he rocked into her palm, she felt her body respond hard, quick, and wet.

"You're not going to leave here without me taking you." He picked her up and took her to the counter. "The others are keeping people away. Monica said it would be her pleasure. But all I can think of is yours. I need you."

"Yes now. Please now." She knew what he'd said; she was in heat. She also knew from talking to the others one evening that being in heat was like a never-ending fuck fest. She couldn't get enough of him, and he would do anything to come inside of her. It lasted an entire week sometimes; Ama told her ten days if she was lucky.

Reed lifted her skirt up, and she felt the cold tile under her seconds later. He was dropping to his knees in front of her when she leaned back against the cool glass. He lifted her legs up to his shoulders and tore her panties from her.

"Come in my mouth. When I drink from you, I want you to come hard and often until I get my fill. Then I'm going to fuck you hard by bending you over this counter and taking you from behind." She nodded, unable to do anything else. "Christ baby, you smell delicious."

He nipped at her clit twice before she came. He'd never get enough of her, and when he lapped hungrily at her, she curled her fingers into his hair and held him to her. Giving her what she wanted, he slid his finger into her and reached deep inside of her until he found the spot that he wanted. When she came this time, she screamed out his name and squeezed him tightly with her thighs. He needed her now.

Standing up, he jerked her to him and took her mouth while he pulled her off the counter. He was aching now, needed to come inside of her like he needed his next breath. And the returning hunger from her made him think she was just as needy. Turning her around, Reed pressed her to the counter so that her face was lying against the surface. Opening his pants, he freed his cock and slammed into her almost in the same instant.

Her scream fueled him. Grabbing her hips, he pulled her toward him with each pound into her. When he looked into the mirror, he saw the most beautiful face in the world. His balls tightened up, and he leaned over. Jerking her blouse down, he bit her.

Blood filled his mouth as she came again, tightening around him until he couldn't move. When she pulled his wrist to her mouth and bit him, he felt his cock release and his balls empty. Christ, he thought as he closed his eyes at the sensations. He was going to die just like this.

Lying over her, he felt her giggle. His body was spent, but the feel of her so happy had his cock stirring again.

Telling him to behave, he pushed the hair off her face and looked down at her. She smiled up at him.

"Is it going to be like this the entire time I'm in heat?" He kissed her gently and lifted from her. She moaned when he stepped back, making him want to take her again. "If so, we're going to have to stay home. This could be dangerous for us to be caught with our pants literally down around our ankles."

Reed helped her stand and held her while she regained her equilibrium. When she nodded that she was okay, she stepped back, and he adjusted his pants. He had broken off the button so he had to pull his shirt down over the damage. Handing her the panties he'd torn off her, he laughed when she tossed them into the trash. Reed retrieved them.

"I don't want anyone seeing these and taking them home as a sort of trophy. You're mine." They were moving toward the door to exit the restroom when he felt his brother touch his mind. Khan didn't seem all that happy with him. And his words confirmed it.

You do know that we're all out here waiting on the two of you, don't you? I mean, you couldn't wait until you got her home, or at the very least the limo? Reed laughed. *This is not funny. Do you know how many people are standing around waiting to use the bathroom because they had no idea my little brother couldn't keep his dick in his pants?*

She's in heat. That shut him up. *So, no, I couldn't wait. I want her having my child, and as soon as possible.*

I didn't know. I'm sorry. I've been there, and the police are not – Khan took a deep breath. *Never you mind. Let's just get you two home, shall we?*

They exited the restroom and were engulfed in hugs. His mother avoided Kerry, which surprised him a little. He'd been assured that she'd be able to fix the problem between the two of them. Apparently not. He hugged his mom and held her for just a few minutes when she didn't seem to want to let him go.

"I'm so sorry." He kissed her forehead. "I hurt her so badly and now I can't fix it. I wish I had simply...there are no words I can say to make this up to the two of you."

"Mrs. Bowen? Corrine?" They both turned to Kerry when she stood just behind them. "I'm sorry. I realize how much I hurt you by asking your husband to go with me to the house that day. I should have taken...I should have gone alone."

"You would have died had you not taken him." Kerry didn't answer his mom, which to him said so much. "He saved your life because there was no way that he couldn't. He was an old fool, but he was a good man. A great man. He would never have forgiven himself if you had died that day. I know that now."

"He said that you'd be mad at him. He told me that he loved you very much." His mom nodded and put her head on Reed's shoulder. "George was an honorable man and a great father. I only wish I had known him longer. I'm so sorry."

Kerry started to walk away when his mom pulled her back and held her. Kerry looked at him over her shoulder and mouthed that she loved him. And he felt his heart overflow with it. Stepping to the two women in his life that meant more to him than anything in this world, he hugged them as well. Soon the rest of them joined them. They must have looked ridiculous standing in the middle of a semi-busy airport having a group hug. But right now, all he could think about was that he had them all there and he was so very lucky.

"We need to get home." Khan started moving them to the exit as he spoke. "Camps has made lunch for us all, and I was supposed to have us back there an hour ago."

As they moved to the three limos, Reed found himself sharing one with Kerry and her uncle. The man was very nice, but he kept saying that he needed to talk to them both and wondered if now would be all right.

"I don't know what you think there is to say." Kerry leaned against him as she spoke to her uncle. "I know you want to tell me about my mom, and I've no problem with that, but right now is not a good time. I'm sort of feeling drained right now."

He wanted to laugh when Burton flushed. He had to know, or at least probably guessed, what had happened in the bathroom at the airport. But he only shook his head.

"No. I understand that you're emotionally drained right now. I don't blame you. You've had a lot thrown at you. I wanted to speak to you both about...you're my only family. All I have left of my sister."

Kerry sat up and looked out the window before looking at him again. "I don't want whatever it is you think I should have because of that. I've enough right here with Reed and his family. If you want to be a part of that, I'm okay with that, but I don't want to be any sort of heir to your money."

"That's too bad, sweetheart." Kerry started to speak, but Burton held up his hand. "I have a great deal of money. Not as much as the family has as a whole, but I'm very wealthy. I've had years and years of planning and saving. I've invested very well over the years and have managed to turn a good profit. It's all yours, whether you want it or not."

"Well, I don't." He laughed at her, and Reed had to work hard at not laughing too. She looked as stubborn right now as he'd ever seen her look.

"Too bad. And so you know, you didn't get your stubbornness from your mother. I've got her beat in spades. Also, it's a moot point as of the day I had it confirmed what my heart already knew. You're my only living relative. Also, since you're already being pissy, your eggs have been returned to you."

When she looked like she was going to argue, Reed put his hand over her mouth and held her back. He wasn't positive she'd hurt Burton, but there was no reason to take chances.

"Do you have a problem if she takes the money and uses it for other things? Like setting up college funds for our children? Or donates it to charities to help out?" Burton shook his head and smiled. "Good. I think we can work on her being a lot more thankful for the money."

She took his hand away. "And if I wanted to set up a college fund in the name of someone? Like a fund that would be there for others like me, children who lost their parents and have had to live with less than...desirable people. Can I do that?"

Reed watched the smile come across Burton's face. "You mean a foundation that would support a child or an adult to go to college and not have to worry again? Yes, I think that's an excellent idea. Do you have a name for this foundation?"

"I do. I want to call it the George and Corrine Bowen Foundation, and I know just the person to run it for us. She owes me so much."

CHAPTER 18

"I just don't see why you had to go and name me the person in charge of this thing." Kerry took a deep breath and let it out slowly. She was in too much pain to placate her mother-in-law right now. "You could have named any number of others to this."

"But I didn't want to. I named you." Kerry took another deep breath. "Are you sure this is right?"

"Yes. You're doing fine." She glared at Walker and then looked at Corrine again. "If you want someone to help you, then go for it. Just so long as it's not me. I've enough going on right now with all this other crap he dumped on me."

Her Uncle Burton had died three months ago. He'd not told anyone he'd had a heart condition, not even Rowena. He'd gone to bed one night and had simply not woken up. He'd died with a smile on his face, a face that Kerry wished she could smack right now.

"I've nine, nine," she shouted when another pain ripped through her. "Nine corporations to run, and not a flipping clue how to do it."

"You're doing a fantastic job, love." She glared at Reed, who looked like he just stepped out of a fashion magazine.

"You should have called me sooner and I would have come home then."

"Your brother said it would be hours yet." She looked at Walker when he snickered. "Pay back is going to be a bitch, Walker. I swear to you when this is over, I'm going to make you pay."

Another pain started at her lower back and up through her throat. The scream that tore from her throat hurt her as much as the pain. She looked at Reed when he said her name.

"Breathe, Kerry. Slow and easy. You can do this." She shook her head at him. "Yes, you can. We've been practicing and you know what to do. Just keep breathing for me and we'll get through this."

"I never want to do this again." He nodded at her, and she wanted to punch him in the face. "I swear to you, you're never touching me again."

Walker laughed, then straightened up on his little stool. "Okay, sweetheart. The next time a contraction comes up on you, I want you to bear down like I told you. Take a good hard shit and you'll deliver this little guy."

She felt the tightening again and did just as he'd told her. Bearing down with all her might, she nearly fainted when she felt the relief of the pressure that had built up. She looked at Reed when he laughed.

"It's a boy. We have a son." Reed was handed their son, and she looked over at him when another pain tore from her.

"Walker," she shouted, and he said he had it. Had what, she had no idea, but the urge to push nearly sent her over the edge. When she heard the cry of a baby, she looked down at Walker, who was handing off a baby to the nurse standing next to him. He looked shell-shocked.

"What's wrong? What's happening?" Reed handed the baby in his arms to a nurse, and Kerry thought for sure she was losing it. When Walker told her to bear down again, she knew that something was terribly wrong.

"I can't. I'm too tired. Please, you said it would be over when I pushed before. I can't do this anymore. Just cut it out of me, I beg you."

Walker said something to Reed, and he pulled her face over to look at him. When she looked into his eyes, she didn't see fear but happiness. When he kissed her on the mouth, she started to close her eyes when she had to push again.

Everything was a blur. Babies seemed to be everywhere, and her head was spinning. Corrine kept wiping her face down with a wet cloth, and Reed kept telling her to keep at it. When she closed her eyes after pushing as hard as she could, she felt herself slip away, welcomed it as a matter of fact. Her body felt as if she'd run a marathon on her hands and knees.

When she woke up, she was in a pretty little room with the curtains open. She looked around and found flowers everywhere, as well as people. She looked at Monica when she stood up and walked toward the bed.

"How are you feeling?" Kerry tried to speak, but she was so dry. "Here, Walker said you could have as much as you wanted to drink, and I've had iced tea brought to you. There's two gallons here, so drink as much as you want, but slowly."

She sipped at the straw and felt as if someone had given her a whole new throat. She smiled at Monica when she winked at her. She wanted to sleep again but needed to see the baby.

"Do you think they can bring me our baby? I want to see him. I can hardly keep my eyes open."

"I bet." Monica laughed. "I'll wake the rest of them, and they can hug you before you talk to Reed. You're going to be very surprised, I think."

Kerry had no idea what she meant, but Reed came to her and kissed her. When the door clicked close then opened again, she continued looking at her husband. He kept holding her and kissing her.

"You're beautiful." She shook her head. "Let me be the judge of that, thank you very much. And if I say you are, then you are."

"I love you." He kissed her. "Where's our son? I was so out of it in there, I didn't get to see him. You must think I'm a wuss."

He laughed. "Hardly. Where would you like to start? I've not named them yet, but I thought that—"

"Them?" She sat up when he moved off the bed. There were three little cribs lined up along the wall. She looked at them, then at him.

"You had triplets. All boys, and according to Walker, all identical. I know that we planned to name one of them Burton Reed, but the rest I'm at a loss for."

"Three baby boys." She didn't look at Reed this time; she couldn't take her eyes off the cribs. "Are they all right? I mean three can be...we have three sons?"

"Yes and yes, they're all just fine. All their fingers and toes, and Walker said that they are incredibly healthy. He said that you did a fine job hiding them from him too."

"I didn't know." She glanced at him, then at the cribs, seeing that there were still three there. "Are you going to be all right with this? I mean, we only made up one bed and one...Christ, Reed we have three sons."

"I know. Would you like to meet them?" She nodded, and he moved to the first one and scooped up a baby. She didn't have a clue what to think when he started to hand him to her.

"I've never held a baby before. Well, not my own. And I'm pretty sure it's different than holding someone else's." Reed put the baby in her arms, and she looked down at the little face staring up at her. "Oh my God, Reed, he's beautiful."

"Handsome. And yes, he is. Simply beautiful. Here." He handed her another one on her other side and she looked down at him. This little man had his eyes closed, and he yawned at her. His little lips were so pink, she wanted to kiss them. The third little bundle was held by Reed, but he showed him to her. They were absolutely perfect.

"I'm in love." She started to cry as she looked at them all. "I'm so in love with them, I can hardly contain it. We're so lucky."

"Yes, we are. And Walker said that they are as well. He will be in later to give you and them a once over. But he said we need to come up with names soon. The family is having an argument on which one should be called what." He kissed her gently on her mouth and smiled. "Are you really all right? I was so worried about you."

"I'm perfect now." She kissed Burton on the head and then the other babies. She looked at Reed. "I think I have a solution to our naming problem."

~~~

Corrine held Burton and looked at the other two that had come into the world less than forty-eight hours ago. They were all sleeping now, and she wished one of the others would cry that they needed her so she could hold two in her arms. When Kerry sat in the chair across from her, she smiled.

"Can't get enough of them, can you? I can't. You'd think that they'd be driving us nuts. And I know that it's been only a few hours, but I feel like this is going to be okay." Corrine nodded at her and smiled. "What do you think of their names?"

Corrine felt her eyes tear up. "I couldn't have thought of better names. Naming them...I'm so overwhelmed that you did this."

The first one was called Reed James Bowen the second; the second little man was Burton Olen Bowen; and the little one, the youngest grandson, was Garrett O'Brien Bowen, named after both his grandmothers using their maiden names. Garrett had been George's mother's maiden name, and Corrine's had been O'Brien. She absolutely loved them.

"I didn't know that the maiden names would work so well. I was afraid that one of them would be something like Deatherage or something like that. I went to school with someone with that as a surname, and it was forever being pronounced wrong." Kerry stood up to get little Reed. "We're going to call him James to keep the confusion to a minimum. I don't know if it will last, but at least it might help."

Kerry handed her James and then went back for Garrett. She held him while Corrine held the other two. Corrine was so happy at that moment, she thought for sure she could bust. She nearly ignored the small touch of her mind.

You love them, do you? George sent her his love as he spoke to her from the beyond. *I can't come to see them, but just to know that you love them so much does me well. Another reason that I had to save this one. She's going to do this once more before she and Reed decide they've had enough. Won't stop them from coming later, but the first six will be enough for them for a while.*

Six? Oh my, George, whatever will they do with six little babies? She was secretly excited to know that her son would have so many children. *And do you know what they'll be, by any chance?*

Boys. They'll have six strapping boys like we did. But not one at a time like most. Couldn't have named them better either. Named them after important people. They did the very best. My mom is proud as a pup, she is, and yours…well, I'm thinking she'll need to have her buttons moved to another spot. Been popping them everywhere.

Her mom had been gone for many years, so long that she'd never seen Corrine's children born. She closed her eyes and tried to remember what she looked like, but all she could see was the babies. She glanced at Kerry when she started to nurse Garrett.

Will I see them, George? Do you know that? She kissed the baby in her right arm, then the one on the left. She so wanted to watch them grow into men, but knew that when her time came, she'd be ready to see her George too.

Don't know, love, just don't know. But I can tell you that you'll see most of them come into the world before you're ready to come see me. And don't you go forgetting every little thing they do so we can talk about them all when you come here. Grand place it is here too. You'll love it. Flowers messing the place up at every turn.

He'd always fussed at her about her flowers, but every year he'd buy her flats and flats of them to plant. She decided to keep a notebook with her at all times, and every day she was going to write something about someone in it. Pictures too. She wanted memories for all of them, and that way, she'd have them to share as well.

Good idea. You write it down, and I'll make sure a copy of it is sent up here. You'll leave the thing behind, of course, for them all, but you and I will have a copy too. She loved the idea and decided that she was starting today. *I love you, my Corrine. I miss you terribly. I'll be able to talk to you on occasion, but you can't be telling them. We'll converse, you and I, until the time comes.*

I love you too, you old fool. More and more daily. She looked down at the babies in her arms. *Thank you for what you've given me. All of us. Without you, this would never have been.*

Now don't be going all mushy on me. I did what any man would have done. Course, I did it a great deal better, but I don't want to brag.

Of course he didn't. She smiled when she felt his connection close. He was closed to her, but she knew that if she needed him, he was only a thought away. Helping Kerry move the babies around so she could nurse another, Camps handed her a bottle.

"You'll be staying on for a few more days, Miss Corrine? I'll fix up a room for you if you wish." Kerry nodded at them both. "Very good. I think the family needs you for a time."

Corrine hoped so. She'd never want to intrude, but being here with these children and knowing that all of them were so close to her as well made her feel like she could conquer the world.

About the Author

Kathi Barton, author of the bestselling series Force of Nature, lives in Nashport, Ohio with her husband Paul. In addition to writing full time Kathi likes to spend time with her eight grandkids, three children and three children-in-laws. She writes to relax and have fun.

Her muse, a cross between Jimmy Stewart and Hugh Jackman brings them to life for her readers in a way that has them coming back time and again for more. Her favorite genre is paranormal romance with a great deal of spice. You can visit Kathi on line and drop her an email if you'd like. She loves hearing from her fans. aaronskiss@gmail.com.

Follow Kathi on her blog:
http://kathisbartonauthor.blogspot.com/

www.ingramcontent.com/pod-product-compliance
Lightning Source LLC
Chambersburg PA
CBHW032124170626
46808CB00006B/2090